Praise for

CRYER'S CROSS

"An eerie, gripping, totally addictive, breathtaking whirl of a book with an ending that left me haunted for days. Lisa McMann has done it again—this book is unputdownable!"

—ALYSON NOËL, #1 *New York Times* bestselling
author of the Immortals series.

"A brilliant, engaging, scary piece of fiction. Every word had me sliding closer to the edge of my seat and gripping the cover tighter and tighter. There are books in the world that make you question your reality and the things that go bump in the night—this is one of them."

—HEATHER BREWER, *New York Times* bestselling author
of the Chronicles of Vladmir Tod series

"Part mystery, part ghost story, and part romance, this book has enough to satisfy a variety of readers and will find popularity with McMann's established fan base and new readers alike."

—*Booklist*

"Fans of supernatural thrillers will enjoy this one . . . The present-tense narration gives the story a sense of immediacy."

—*Kirkus Reviews*

"Tragic, emotional, sometimes humorous, and full of tension, *Cryer's Cross* is one stand-out novel and possibly Lisa McMann's best book yet."

—The Compulsive Reader, thecompulsivereader.com

"*Cryer's Cross* is addicting, and a great blend of romance, thrilling plots, and paranormal activity to keep you up at night. A must read!"

—twilightseriestheories.com

"An exciting page-turner of a thriller that fans will not want to see end, leaving them impatiently waiting for McMann's next book."

—teenreads.com

ALSO BY LISA McMANN

Wake

Fade

Gone

CRYER'S CROSS

LISA McMANN

SIMON PULSE
NEW YORK LONDON TORONTO SYDNEY NEW DELHI

For Kennedy

SIMON PULSE
An imprint of Simon & Schuster Children's Publishing Division
1230 Avenue of the Americas, New York, NY 10020
First Simon Pulse paperback edition December 2011. Copyright © 2011 by Lisa McMann. All rights reserved, including the right of reproduction in whole or in part in any form. SIMON PULSE and colophon are registered trademarks of Simon & Schuster, Inc. For information about special discounts for bulk purchases, please contact Simon & Schuster Special Sales at 1-866-506-1949 or business@simonandschuster.com. The Simon & Schuster Speakers Bureau can bring authors to your live event. For more information or to book an event contact the Simon & Schuster Speakers Bureau at 1-866-248-3049 or visit our website at www.simonspeakers.com. Designed by Mike Rosamilia and Karina Granda.
The text of this book was set in Janson Text.
Manufactured in the United States of America
2 4 6 8 10 9 7 5 3 1
The Library of Congress has cataloged the hardcover edition as follows:
McMann, Lisa. Cryer's Cross / by Lisa McMann. — 1st Simon Pulse hardcover ed. p. cm. Summary: Seventeen-year-old Kendall, who suffers from obsessive-compulsive disorder, lives with her parents on a potato farm in a tiny community in Montana, where two teenagers go missing within months of each other, with no explanation. [1. Obsessive-compulsive disorder—Fiction. 2. Supernatural—Fiction. 3. Missing children—Fiction. 4. Interpersonal relations—Fiction. 5. Montana— Fiction. 6. Mystery and detective stories.]
I. Title.   PZ7.M478757Cr 2011   [Fic]—dc22   2010015410
ISBN 978-1-4169-9482-4 (pbk)
ISBN 978-1-4169-9481-7 (hc) ISBN 978-1-4424-3608-4 (eBook)

ACKNOWLEDGMENTS

Many thanks:

To my daughter, Kennedy, for all the incredibly tough challenges she's endured with her OCD, and for letting me share some of it in hopes that others might understand or find some comfort. I'm really proud of you, kiddo.

To my son, Kilian, for being one of my first readers, and for his discerning artist's eye. Also for being the front.

To my amazing husband, Matt, my biggest supporter, who constantly picks up the slack without complaint when I'm traveling or on deadline, and who reads everything I write, even when it's rough, and helps me make it better.

To the White House Boys for telling their story and inspiring part of this one.

To Kendall Kovalik, for whom the main character is named, and her lovely mom who donated so generously to Project Book Babe to make it happen.

To Dave Gritter and Lindy Flanigan for your help with all the soccer stuff.

To June and Karl DeJonge for knowing so much about potato farms in Montana.

To Deke Snow for carrying my luggage to my room in Rochester and for being generally awesome in all ways.

To my agent, Michael Bourret, for the encouragement, the thoughtfulness, the never-ending hard work, and the laughs. You are one amazing person. I am so grateful for everything you have done for me.

To my editor, Jennifer Klonsky, who jumped on my extremely primitive idea for this book before I even knew it was an idea, and to the entire team at Simon Pulse for all you do for me and for my books. You guys are incredible and I love you and appreciate you so much.

To all the AYT actors I've met over the years—you have been such awesome readers and spreaders of the book love. Thanks for telling your friends! And always remember that I am your biggest fan.

CRYER'S CROSS

WE

When it is over, We breathe and ache like old oak, like peeling birch. One of Our lost souls set free. We move, a chess piece in the dark room, cast-iron legs a centimeter at a time, crying out in silent carved graffiti. Calling to Our next victim, Our next savior. We carve on Our face:

Touch me.
Save my soul.

ONE

Everything changes when Tiffany Quinn disappears.

Of the 212 residents of Cryer's Cross, Montana, 178 join Sheriff Greenwood in a search that lasts several days from sunup to after dark. School is closed, all the students taking part, searching roads and farms, trudging through pastures of cattle and horses, through sections of newly planted potatoes, barley, wheat. Up to the foothills and back along the woods. They travel in groups of two or three, some nervous, some crying, some resolute. Shouting to the other groups now and then so nobody else goes missing—cell phones aren't much good out here. Cryer's Cross is a dead spot.

After five days there is still no trace of Tiffany Quinn.

She is gone, impossibly. Impossibly, because to imagine that there has been foul play here in the humble town of Cryer's Cross is laughable, and to imagine that sweet ninth-grade bookworm running away, going off on her own . . . It's all so impossible.

But gone she is.

Still, they search.

Kendall Fletcher flinches and casts regular glances behind her out of habit. Scared about the younger girl's disappearance, true, but also unsettled by this shake-up in her schedule. The final week of her junior year canceled—everything left unfinished, open ended. Her whole routine is off.

She walks the hundreds of acres of her parents' farm and beyond into the woods, wearily counting her steps through the potatoes and grain fields and trees. Counting, always counting something.

Her best friend, Nico Cruz, walks next to her.

Boyfriend, he'd say.

But boyfriend means commitment, and commitments that she can't keep tend to make Kendall feel prickly. "Come on," she says. "Let's run."

She takes off through the field, and Nico follows. They pass an imaginary soccer ball between the rows, occasionally yelling out "Tiffany!" Once, after they cross over to Nico's family's land, they see a big brown lump where the barley field meets the gravel road, but it's not Tiffany. Just a road-killed deer.

She's not here. She's not anywhere.

They take a break under a tree at the edge of the farm as rain starts to fall. Kendall stares and counts the drops as they hit the gray dirt, faster and faster.

Nico talks, but Kendall isn't listening. She needs to get to a hundred drops before she can allow herself to stop.

Eventually the search ends. Nothing more can be done locally except by professionals now. It's prime planting season. Farmers have chores, and students do too. Plus jobs, if they work in town or for one of the farmers or ranchers. Life has to go on.

It's a long, hot summer full of hard work for Kendall. For everyone. After a month or two, people stop talking about Tiffany Quinn.

TWO

In September when school starts again, Kendall arrives as she always does, the first one to the one-room high school, except for old Mr. Greenwood, the part-time janitor, who retreats to his basement hideout whenever students are around.

Kendall is tan and not quite freakishly tall. Athletic. Her long brown hair has natural highlights from her driving a tractor and working on the farm all summer.

There was too much time to think up there on that tractor, since all it takes is a GPS to run it up and down the rows. And when your brain has a glitch and its lap counter is broken, the same thoughts whir around on an endless loop. Tiffany Quinn. Tiffany Quinn. Tiffany Quinn.

Kendall imagines every possible scenario for Tiffany. Running away. Getting lost. Being abducted. Maybe even raped, murdered. Wondering which one really happened, and if they'll ever know the truth. She pictures all of it happening to herself, and it almost makes her cry. Pictures Tiffany screaming for help, begging to live . . . Kendall's eyes blur as she remembers her summer, turning the tractor through the fields and obsessing about such horrible things. It seemed so real, so scary, as if someone were about to jump out of the woods and attack her.

She knows some of her thoughts are irrational. She knows it and always has known it, even in fifth grade, when she used to layer on clothes—four shirts, three pairs of underwear, shorts under her jeans—anxiously, frantically, crying her eyes out for fear people could see her naked through her clothes. What an awful time that was. Fear like that is constant, tiring. But the psychologist over in Bozeman helped. Explained OCD—obsessive-compulsive disorder—and eventually that particular phase of worry went away, only to be replaced by other obsessions, other compulsions.

She's not crazy. She just can't stop thinking things when weird ideas get lodged in her head. She also can't stop glancing behind her—it has become her latest compulsion. This whole thing with Tiffany has set her back some.

So she's glad to be back at school, though feeling a little desperate because of how last year ended. And anxious to start this year fresh. Anxious to have new thoughts, new assignments bombard her brain, keep her mind occupied with non-scary things. Soccer practice starting up again. New DVD dance routines to learn. New things to keep her busy, body and mind. It's a relief.

On this first day she tidies up the classroom in a way that old Mr. Greenwood doesn't, turning the wastebasket so the dent is in the right place, straightening the markers on the dry-erase board and putting them in color order to match Roy G Biv as closely as possible, opening the curtains just so. Lining up the desks into their proper places in neat quadrants, one quadrant of six desks for each high school grade. Kendall creates aisles separating the quadrants to give the teacher room to walk between them, so she can address each grade individually rather than having all twenty-four desks together. It's the way Kendall likes things.

Nobody's ever complained.

Nobody even knows.

The desks are ancient and sturdy beasts from the 1950s, recycled by the state from who knows where. It's a workout moving them all, but Kendall feels better when everything is back to normal. She sees where her old desk ended up, over in the freshman quadrant this year. Now the tenth graders will have an empty seat, unless the rumors are true. There's a new family in town, according to Nico, though Kendall hasn't seen anyone new around town yet. Kendall hopes they have a sophomore to fill the spot left by Tiffany, to make things in that section neat again. Though Tiffany coming back would be the best thing, of course. But Sheriff Greenwood and the local news anchors say that's just not likely. Not after all this time has passed.

Kendall opens the curtains wide enough so that the edges of them hang in line with the sides of the windows. Her irrational fear gets the better of her and she checks the window locks, first struggling to open the windows to make sure the locks are sturdy, then running her forefinger over each lock in the same manner. "All checked and good," she says. No one is there to hear her, but she has to say it out loud or it doesn't count.

When she sees students walking up the yard to the little school, Kendall looks over her handiwork. The door creaks open. Kendall moves to her new desk in the senior quadrant, takes out an antiseptic wipe from her book bag, and cleans her desk quickly before anybody can see and make fun. She's not a compulsive hand-washer, like some. But she likes to know the germ status of her own personal work space at the beginning of a school year. Doesn't everybody?

Nico spies her and comes over. His straight white-blond hair hangs in his eyes. He's got his father's Spanish name but his mother's Dutch looks. Nico swishes his hair aside and gives Kendall a half grin. Throws his book bag onto the floor and shoves his body into the desk just to the right of Kendall. "These desks aren't getting any bigger," he mutters, trying to fit his knees under the metal basin. He leans over and pecks Kendall on the cheek. "Hey. Sorry I was late. You want to go up to Bozeman this Saturday?"

"What for?"

"I gotta look at Montana State. Check out the nursing school."

The guy behind them snickers. "Nurse Nico."

"Shut it, Brandon," Nico says in a calm voice. He whips his arm back without looking, and it connects with the side of Brandon's head.

"Sure," Kendall says. "I want to check out their theatre and dance program, just in case."

Nico flashes a sympathetic smile. "Still no word?"

"No." The chances of a rural girl with very little formal training in theatre or dance getting into Juilliard are probably less than zero, but Kendall sees no reason not to start at the top.

Kendall idly counts bodies as everyone else files in. She subtracts last year's seniors and Tiffany Quinn, and adds the incoming freshmen. Ms. Hinkler explains the seating arrangement to the freshmen, new to this building. She also announces to the noisy room that there will be two new students this year, which is practically unheard of.

The rumor of the new family must be true. Cryer's Cross is, apparently, a boom town.

"Looks like it'll be a full house this year," Kendall murmurs. Twenty-four students. Perfection.

The two new students enter the room and everyone watches curiously. Ms. Hinkler checks them in and assigns them seats. She directs one of the new students to the senior section. He looks beyond Kendall and frowns.

"Hey," Kendall says when he stops at the only empty desk, to the left of hers.

The guy mutters something, but he doesn't look at her. He sits down and puts his backpack on the floor under his desk.

Nico leans over Kendall's desk. "Hey. I'm Nico. How's it going?"

The guy nods, almost imperceptibly, but remains silent.

Nico raises his eyebrow.

Kendall laughs. "Okay, then," she says. "This should be fun." She studies the new guy. He's tough-looking and muscular. Medium-brown skin, his hair black and wavy. His clothes aren't anything special, but they're clean and neat. His shoes are dusty like everyone else's. Cryer's Cross could use some rain.

The other new student, a sophomore girl, has brown skin too, with a spattering of darker freckles across her nose and cheeks. Black wavy hair. They're both striking. "Is that your sister?" Kendall asks.

The new guy closes his eyes, feigning sleep, arms crossed over his chest. Kendall sighs. She turns her attention to her new desk, reading the graffiti. But it's already familiar—she's been reading and memorizing desk graffiti for years now. She knows every desk by heart. She can't help it. It's one of those OCD things.

Being Kendall is exhausting.

Once Ms. Hinkler has all the freshmen students checked in, she introduces them to the rest of the class. Like everyone else, Kendall pretty much knows them all. Some of their parents work on the Fletchers' potato farm. But all eyes are on the transfer students. They are introduced, brother and sister indeed. The girl is Marlena and the guy is Jacián Obregon. Ms. Hinkler stumbles over his name.

"Not JAY-se-un," he says, suddenly awake again. "Hah-see-AHN."

Ms. Hinkler blushes. "My apologies." She repeats it the right way. Jacián Obregon. It sounds like a melody. Or a tragedy.

It's a boisterous, testosterone-filled day for Kendall, wedged between Nico and Jacián, with stupid Brandon directly behind her and two more guys on either side of him—Travis Shank, and Eli Greenwood, who is the son of the sheriff and grandson of the janitor. It's always been like this. Kendall's the only girl her age in the entire town. It figures that when they finally get a new kid in her grade, it's another guy.

But Nico's there like always. He's been her best friend ever since they were babies. He knows about Kendall's OCD, understands it, and it doesn't bother him at all. Best guy in the world? Kendall thinks so. She gives him a wide smile when she passes the syllabus to him.

At lunch Kendall and Nico trade sandwiches like they've done every day since kindergarten, except when Nico brings tuna salad, which Kendall can't stand. They eat together in the grass, talking about college options and how it's going to suck to be apart.

After school Kendall and Nico head to soccer practice out in the field behind the building. Soccer here is coed and all varsity since there aren't enough high school girls in Cryer's Cross to make up a girls' team, and there aren't enough students who want to play soccer to have a JV team as well. Kendall's the only girl to stick it out. And she's better than most of the guys.

As Kendall finishes stretching, Jacián shows up to the field, dressed in Nike soccer apparel like they're sponsoring him or something. Kendall jogs in place, rubber band between her teeth, and whips her hair into a ponytail as she watches him walk. She can tell he's an athlete. She says his

name to herself so she doesn't forget how to pronounce it—
not a lot of Jaciáns around here.

A moment later Marlena appears, dressed for practice
in less obvious designer sportswear. She sees Jacián and
runs toward him.

Kendall stares. "They're both playing?" she says under
her breath to Nico.

"Looks that way." Nico grabs a ball from the ball bag
and tosses it at the ground in front of Kendall, who cap-
tures it with her foot and dribbles automatically away from
the others.

"Well, we definitely have room on the team." They
pass the ball back and forth. Kendall thinks of the four
team members they lost to graduation last year.

"Yeah, there's too much room, and only one freshman
that I know of wants to join us. And this new girl. I suppose Coach will take anybody with a pulse. But we're still
short. How many is that, number girl?"

"Eight," Kendall says automatically.

"Yowch." He scratches his head. "I hope Coach can
recruit a few more, or we're going to be killing ourselves
playing against full teams."

Kendall squints and shrugs. "We're not the only team
with low numbers. We can do it with eight. Though it'll
be hell playing Bozeman teams with the full eleven." She
watches the Obregons stretch, waiting to see what they

can do. "You know, it might be nice having another girl around," she says finally. "Jacián, on the other hand . . . Well, I guess it won't make a difference."

When Jacián plows into Kendall during a four-on-four practice scrimmage and leaves her with the wind knocked out of her, though, she realizes he actually might make a difference. "Asshole," she mutters when she gets her wind back. "Coach, hello! That was a foul." She gets back up and runs to help protect her goal, but it's too late. Jacián scores against her team.

THREE

After practice Kendall follows Marlena to the tiny girls' locker room, which is more of a lean-to against the school building than anything else. "You guys are good," Kendall says.

Marlena smiles. "Thanks. Jacián is great. I'm just okay." Her voice is warm and rich.

"You're way better than Brandon," Kendall says, feeling generous.

"Which one is he?"

"The immature senior loser with the light brown hair. Kinda big and dopey, about this tall." She holds up her hand to about six feet four. "He sits behind me in school. I'm sure you know who I mean. The guy who didn't actually manage to touch the ball the entire scrimmage but fell down multiple times."

"Yeah. I think so." She grins.

They strip down, clean up, and change back into street clothes, layering on deodorant. Couldn't shower even if they wanted to, but there's a sink at least. "So," Kendall says, "what's your brother's problem?"

Marlena raises an eyebrow. "What do you mean?"

"He's not very friendly. Hasn't said a word."

"Oh, that. He's just upset," Marlena says. She lowers her voice, even though it's just the two of them. "He doesn't really want to be here."

"Why not?"

Marlena shrugs. "Moving away from all his friends for his senior year. Leaving his girlfriend, trying to do a long-distance-relationship thing. And then when we got here . . . Well, you probably know."

"Know what?"

"About the sheriff coming over. Right when we moved in. Everybody seems to know everybody else's business here."

Kendall shakes her head. "I don't know. I was isolated on a tractor twelve hours a day all summer. What happened?"

Marlena pulls a makeup bag from her backpack and starts applying eyeliner. "Well, we moved here in May, right after our school year was done down in Arizona. Right before that girl Tiffany disappeared, I guess. Sheriff Greenwood and the state police thought maybe Jacián had something to do with it."

Kendall's eyes widen. Her heart skips, and the irrational fear wells up. "Oh. . . ." The word gets caught in her throat, and bad thoughts start looping.

"He didn't, though, obviously. After a while the sheriff stopped bugging him." Marlena scowls as she swipes her lips with gloss. "Jacián was really pissed off, though. Called the sheriff a racist."

Kendall swallows hard. "So . . . why did you guys move here?"

"My grandfather." She replaces the cap and fishes around in her makeup bag. "He's getting older, and his business wasn't doing very well. He's not keeping up with technology. Still uses horses to round up cattle. Can you believe that? My mother and father decided to come here and take care of things. Family is a big deal to them. To all of us." Marlena turns to look at Kendall. "Are you all right?"

Kendall stops staring at Marlena and turns on the faucet, washes her hands, stares at the water instead. "Wait . . . so, who's your grandfather? I don't know any Obregons around here."

"It's my mother's father. Hector Morales. A mile down RR-4."

Kendall grins. "Oh, Hector's Farm! Everybody loves him. We buy lots of stuff from him—milk, beef. I didn't know he was having trouble." Somehow, Marlena and Jacián being related to Hector makes them a little less scary.

"It's not too bad, my mother says. He's just not able to keep up with beef orders as well as he used to, and he lost some cattle over the winter. Plus, he's too stubborn to hire help, so I guess he lost some commercial business. We're trying to get it back."

"Well, we'll keep buying all our stuff from you guys, I'm sure. And the cool thing is you can ride. He's got beautiful stables. You can even ride to school if you want. There's a hitching post over on the side of the building."

"No way, really?" Marlena grins and picks up her backpack. "This place is so old-fashioned. We rode back home too, but just for fun. It's in the blood, I think. We'll be switching Grandpa over to four-wheelers soon." Somebody outside the building pounds on the wall, and Marlena startles.

"That'll be Nico," Kendall says. She grabs her bag. "Nice getting to know you."

Marlena smiles. "Don't let my brother get to you. He's just pretty mad about everything right now."

"No kidding," Kendall says. She pushes the door open and comes face-to-face with Jacián Obregon.

He glares.

She glares back, but her stomach twists. "You fouled me," she says.

He doesn't speak for a moment. When he does, his voice is lower than she expects. "Stay out of my way, then, if you don't want to get hurt." He dismisses Kendall by the mere act of looking beyond her, to Marlena. "Come on, Lena," he says sharply. He turns in the dirt and starts walking toward the parking area.

Marlena smiles an apology to Kendall and takes off after Jacián. "See you tomorrow," she calls out.

Kendall waves halfheartedly at Marlena as Nico walks up. "He's a jerk."

Nico nods. "Yep. Pretty much."

Kendall smiles and starts walking. "Let's go. I've got chores and homework. Felt good to play again, though, didn't it?"

"It was awesome. You get hurt at all?"

"No. I can take it. . . ." She trails off.

"What?"

Kendall looks over her shoulder as they cross the dirt road and cut the corner of a barley field. "Marlena said they moved here right before Tiffany disappeared, and that Eli's dad suspected Jacián might have had something to do with it."

"What? That's crazy."

"Is it? I mean, how would we know? He's mean. Maybe he's unstable."

"Kendall."

"Seriously, what if he has her all tied up in the woods. Or maybe he chopped her up into little pieces. . . ."

"Kendall, stop it. That's ridiculous."

She's not convinced.

They walk until they reach the halfway point between their respective family farms—directly across the road from each other. For a moment they stand in the middle of the road facing each other and holding hands. Nico leans in and kisses her sweetly.

"Don't work too hard," Nico says.

"You either. Call me at eleven?"

"Always."

Kendall smiles, and they part company, each down their long driveways.

FOUR

At home Kendall throws her backpack onto the big oak kitchen table. "Hi, Mom," she sings, and gives her mother a kiss on the cheek.

"How was your first day?" Mrs. Fletcher stands at the sink watering her herb garden. She's tall and dark-haired like Kendall, wearing capri jeans and a red-checked short-sleeved shirt, knotted at her waist.

"Fine."

"Was it hard without Tiffany there?"

"Yeah, a little. Everybody noticed but nobody said anything—pretty much what I figured."

"How's the OCD? Do you feel a little better now that you're back into the school routine?"

Kendall breaks off a piece of a bran muffin and shoves it into her mouth. "Immensely. Shit, I'm starving."

"Honey. Inside language, please."

"Sorry. Man, I'm starving. Better?"

"Yes. What else is new? Did you meet Hector's grand-kids?"

Kendall tilts her head. "You know about them?"

"They've been around for a couple months."

"Why am I the last to know everything?"

"I didn't know you didn't know. The girl's been sitting at their market stand all summer. Such a striking young woman."

"Well, I've been on that damn tractor all summer, watching my leg muscles atrophy. I'm all wobbly."

"Language, Kendall."

"Sorry. Got used to farm talk again. Maybe you shouldn't make me work so hard with all those swearers."

Mrs. Fletcher looks like she's trying not to grin. "I know. But the work is good for you. Builds character."

Kendall rolls her eyes and pulls the milk jug from the refrigerator. Its label reads FRESH AS HECK FROM HECTOR FARMS. How could anybody not adore Hector Morales? She pours an impossibly large tumbler full and drinks it all. Slams it on the counter, empty. "Any mail?"

"Nothing from Juilliard."

Kendall screws up her nose, disappointed. "Okay.

Well, what needs to get done before I start practicing?"

"Dad's checking the southwest field today to see how close we're getting to harvest. He wants you out there to show you how he does that. Then dinner. Then homework. Then you can practice."

"Big sigh, Mummy," Kendall says. "I am so sick of potatoes, I could scream."

"Another six weeks and it'll all be pretty near over."

Kendall starts jogging to the field, but the milk sloshes in her stomach and her thighs burn from the soccer scrimmage, so she slows down to a walk. Even out here, on her home turf, Kendall feels uneasy walking alone. She heads for the southwest field, looking nervously over her shoulder every thirty paces or so.

After a few minutes she hears her father's familiar yell and catches up to him. "Hey, Daddy!"

"How's my girl?" Mr. Fletcher air-hugs Kendall. His hands are filthy.

"Good, now that I'm with you," she says, demure. "Whatcha got?"

"This here is what we call a potato," Mr. Fletcher says.

"Fascinating."

They walk the field together a few rows apart, stopping now and then to check for ripeness, rot, and bugs. Kendall's mind wanders, remembering earlier in the day, picking up random thoughts to obsess over.

"Machines are good," Mr. Fletcher says, taking on a teaching tone, "but they don't compare to the human eye, or the touch of a hand. That's the real way to keep crops, to be one with them, to create potatoes that love you back."

"Yeppers," Kendall says, but she's not paying attention. She's picturing Jacián sneaking off to kidnap, murder, and chop poor innocent girls into pieces.

By the time she gets her homework done, it's nine thirty p.m. and her legs ache, but she's not done. She slips a DVD into the player and sits down on her bedroom floor to stretch and warm up. By nine forty-five she's running through ballet positions, and then she works into her routine, the one she choreographed herself for the Juilliard application video. It feels good. But she's exhausted.

By the time Nico calls her phone line at eleven to say goodnight, she's already asleep. But it's a good sleep. Being busy and exhausted is about the best thing for Kendall's brain.

She even forgot to check her window lock six times.

WE

Thirty-five. One hundred. Thirty-five. One hundred. We know. The weight, the heat. There is life heavy against Us again. A heartbeat, a pulse through taut skin.

Please.
Help me.

FIVE

In the morning Kendall rises at six. She gets online and looks up the youth theatre in Bozeman, wondering what productions they're doing this fall and if there would possibly be time to squeeze in a play on top of soccer and life. Last spring she got the part of Miss Dorothy in *Thoroughly Modern Millie*. It was the most fun Kendall has had in her entire life. The director called her a natural, and she even got nominated for a local youth theatre award. Not bad for her first musical.

But Kendall has always known she wants to sing, dance, act. She's been doing it on her own since she was a little kid, always doing productions in the barn, using cats as her other actors if she couldn't talk Nico, Eli, Travis, or even stupid Brandon into participating.

Nico usually played along. He is the closest neighbor, and their mothers have been friends since before Kendall and Nico were born. Nico was agreeable to doing almost anything Kendall requested, except when it came to singing or dancing, which Kendall thought was probably good, since he's terrible at both.

Kendall pulls up the theatre's website and sees they are auditioning for *Grease*. She scans the rehearsal schedule but knows it's impossible. She can't drive all the way out to Bozeman multiple times a week during harvest and soccer season. Too far away. Too many conflicts.

Too many stupid potatoes.

She checks her e-mail and then closes her laptop and gets ready for school.

At school things are pretty much just as they were yesterday. Kendall turns the wastebasket, straightens the markers, opens the curtains, tugs to check the windows, and runs her fingers over each window lock. "All checked and good," she whispers. Then she makes minor adjustments to the desks.

She watches the students arrive, many of them walking, some driving cars or pickup trucks. Kendall tries to see Cryer's Cross through the eyes of a newcomer like

Marlena. Some of the students wear cowboy hats and boots, others wear Gap or Levi's or Target or home sewn. It's not that strange, she guesses.

When Nico comes walking up to the school, Kendall smiles. She's really proud of him wanting to be a nurse. He's been bandaging cats and farm animals since the two of them were little. The other guys aren't jerks about it like Brandon.

The school day progresses. Ms. Hinkler assigns the upper-classmen various things to read and work on, and then she spends the most time with the freshmen, which she'll do for this first week, until they get used to her and how things work.

In the senior section Brandon and Travis sleep. Eli Greenwood reads for a while, then jiggles his leg and doodles in the margins of his English book. Jacián does trigonometry problems on scratch paper until his work is done, and then he slumps in his seat and traces his finger over the desk graffiti. Nico props his head up with one arm and rests the other on the desk next to his open physics textbook. His eyes close. Kendall pretends to read, but she's daydreaming about Broadway.

There is something about performing that soothes Kendall's overactive brain. It's like the concentration necessary for acting takes the attention away from the never-ending circle of thoughts that drives her sometimes irrational behavior. And she wants it—she wants that relief. That control over her list of obsessions and compulsions. Maybe this winter she can do another show once soccer and potatoes are done. Maybe.

In the sophomore section Marlena glances over her shoulder, catches Kendall's eye, and smiles.

At noon everybody heads outside to eat lunch or hit the locker rooms for a bathroom break. Some go home for lunch if they live close to town. Nico and Kendall live just a little too far away to make that worthwhile.

"Bored yet?" Kendall lies down on her back in the grass next to Nico. It's a beautiful day, a few clouds, maybe seventy-five degrees.

Nico is quiet. Kendall pokes him.

"Hmm?"

"I asked if you were bored yet. With school."

With visible effort he pulls himself from his thoughts. "Oh. No. I think I'm going to like physics."

"I wish we had more options. You know. Ceramics. Drama."

Nico rolls to his side and looks at Kendall. Touches her cheek. "Me too, for you. No mail?"

"Nope."

"Good." Nico falls back again. "I don't want you to go."

Kendall laughs and punches him in the shoulder. "Stop! You'll jinx Juilliard."

"I know. I'm sorry. I just wish you weren't going to be way out in New York . . . I haven't gone a whole week in my entire life without seeing you—since before you were born."

"Well, maybe you should consider coming out that way too. Why do I have to be the one to stay around here?"

Nico winces. "You're right."

"Of course I am." She sits up. Closes her eyes and sighs. "But the truth is, I'm not going to get into Juilliard, and we both know it. So. Saturday I'm checking out State with you."

Nico grins. "Awesome."

Back in the classroom, though, Nico acts distracted. He rests his head on his desk, eyes half closed.

Kendall pokes him when Ms. Hinkler is working with the sophomores. "Are you okay?"

Nico turns slowly to look at Kendall, a faraway look in his eyes. "Fine," he says. He faces forward once again, his fingers sliding across the edge of his desk.

"You're acting really strange."

"Shh," Nico says, distracted. He shakes his head slightly and doesn't answer further. Then he puts his head back down and closes his eyes.

* * *

At soccer practice Coach works the team hard. They run drills and suicide competitions. It's hard work, but Kendall savors it. It keeps her mind busy. But as she runs, something Jacián said yesterday keeps repeating in her mind, a syllable with every step. *Stay out of my way, then, if you don't want to get hurt.*

Did Jacián say that to Tiffany Quinn, too, before he killed her? Kendall shakes her head, admonishing herself in jagged whispers as she runs the suicide drills. She glances at him. *Stop it. Stop it. Stop it. Just run.*

She beats everybody. It's never happened before, but Kendall's in her groove today. Jacián comes in second. Eli is third, with Marlena grabbing his shirt trying to pass him, but she ends up fourth. Nico's off his game, coming in seventh out of the eight. Jacián walks away, gasping for breath.

Kendall smiles triumphantly before half the team shoves her onto the ground and piles on top. She gasps and laughs, trying to shield her face from kicking legs and waving arms. Briefly catches Jacián's eye as he stands a few feet away, watching the congratulatory pileup. His eyes burn holes into hers. She flails and turns, and sees Nico, but he's staring off at nothing.

In a minute she wriggles out from under the pile as Coach yells for everybody to get back to work.

* * *

At 11:05 p.m. Kendall calls Nico. "What's up with you?"

"Huh?"

"You missed the call. You almost never miss the call."

"Oh. Uh . . . I lost track of time, I guess. Got a lot on my mind."

"You want to talk about it? Please? You're starting to worry me."

"No. No, thanks. I have to go."

"Okaaay. . . ."

"Good night, Kendall."

Kendall pulls the phone from her ear and stares at it for a second, and then puts it back up to her ear again. "Are you kidding me?"

But all she hears is a dial tone. Her stomach twists. Nico hung up on her. "Damn, boy," she says. "This college thing must be huge for you, that's all I can say." She calls his private line again. Five times.

All she gets is a busy signal.

She checks her lock six times and then stares through the window, out over the front fields. Toward Nico's house.

All is dark.

Kendall shivers.

WE

*Touch Our face and you'll hear Us again. You'll wonder.
You'll let Us into your mind, your thoughts. Your soul. We
whisper to you in a single melting voice—the voice you want
to hear. You know that voice. You miss it.*

You want to save it.

SIX

The first week of school nears an end. The unspeakable absence of Tiffany Quinn is mostly forgotten, replaced by new assignments, new students, and a need for life to be normal. Kendall performs her morning routines—the wastebasket, the markers, the windows, the desks—and things are good. Mostly.

Jacián still doesn't speak in class unless Ms. Hinkler asks him a question.

And Nico is completely lost in his own world, oblivious to Kendall.

He won't discuss it.

Her brain goes into overdrive.

* * *

"Nico," she says at lunch, outside on the grass. "Is it me? Is it something I did?"

He stares at the sky. His lips move, but no words come out.

"Nico?"

He turns to look at Kendall. "What?"

Kendall bites her lip, and tears spring to her eyes. "What's wrong with you? Monday you were normal, and now everything's really weird."

He just shakes his head. "Nothing."

"Are we still going to Bozeman tomorrow?"

"Bozeman. . . . Oh, yeah. Yeah, sure."

"Are you mad at me or something?"

He stares for a minute as if he's trying to comprehend the question, and then he takes her hand. "No, baby. I love you. Like always." He looks into her eyes and brings her hand to his lips. But his look is vacant. He kisses her knuckles, drops her hand, gets to his feet, and walks back into the school.

There's no soccer practice on Fridays—not until games actually begin. Nico starts home after school without Kendall. She watches him, incredulous, and then she turns and walks up the street into town.

The town portion of Cryer's Cross consists of one

four-way-stop intersection with a handful of stores, a restaurant, and a big indoor farmers' market that doubles for whatever else might require a large organized space throughout the year. Kendall climbs the steps to the drugstore, in desperate need of tampons.

Outside the building is a porch with an awning, and under the awning, sitting in aged wooden chairs, are old Mr. Greenwood and Hector Morales. Kendall grins and waves. The two men often sit together in the early evenings during good weather, not talking, just sitting. Old Mr. Greenwood is grouchy, but Hector brightens up when he sees Kendall.

"Miss Kendall," Hector says. "Come here, please."

Kendall goes over to the men. "Yes, sir?"

"You are a good friend to Marlena at school. Thank you for that. You hear me?"

Kendall smiles. Hector is such a sensitive man, so kind. She wonders how his offspring could have produced somebody so awful as Jacián. "Marlena's a great girl," Kendall says. "Really good at soccer."

"And Jacián, he is our soccer champion," Hector says with a proud chuckle.

"Yes," Kendall says, trying to sound enthusiastic. "Yes, he's really talented."

"He needs the friends too," Hector says, a little softer, but somehow with more punch. "People need friends."

He glances at Mr. Greenwood, who shifts uncomfortably. "You're a good girl. You give him a chance, okay?"

"Okay," Kendall says. What else can she say? "I'll try." And before she can help it, she adds, "And he should give everybody else a chance too."

Hector looks thoughtfully at Kendall, his finger on his lips as he thinks. "I agree, Miss Kendall. You are wise for someone so young, and I thank you."

Kendall can't help smiling. She reaches and takes his hand, holds it for a minute. "Good to see you again."

She goes inside the shop and wanders around, looking at things. Thinking about Nico, and wondering what's really going on with him.

Then she pays and walks the mile home, looking over her shoulder every thirty paces. Walking alone always reminds her of Tiffany Quinn.

Kendall does her chores and homework, mopes about Nico but is glad they'll have a chance to talk things out tomorrow on the way to Bozeman. Her parents say good night and turn in. By ten thirty Kendall falls asleep on the couch watching music videos.

WE

You lay your cheek against Ours and whisper, "Who are you?" We feel your heart, your quickening breath. Your pulsing blood. Yes, We hear you. And We know what to do. Soothe. Beckon. Tempt. Capture, oh yes. We capture you. From the first touch, We had you.

Come back tonight.
Save me!
Say nothing!

SEVEN

Kendall wakes up to the doorbell ringing. Once, twice. Bright sunshine streams in through the living room curtains—she slept on the couch all night. *Crap*, she thinks. *Overslept. Bozeman today.* She goes to the door in her pajamas.

It's not Nico.

It's Jacián. With a side of beef.

"Delivery," he says. He's wearing dark sunglasses, and Kendall can't see his eyes. She grips the placket of her pajama top in residual fifth-grade fear.

"Oh." She moves out of the way as he brings a box inside. She wonders briefly if she has morning breath. If it were anyone else at the door, she might actually care.

"Freezer?" He shifts his weight from one foot to the other.

"Downstairs. . . . Here." Kendall runs her fingers through her tangled bed-head and leads him to the basement door, down the steps. It's cool down here. Smells like rain and dirt. She opens the freezer door and hurriedly rearranges the containers of sweet corn she and her mother prepared and froze last month. She puts them into neat rows, stacking them just right.

"This is heavy," Jacián says.

Kendall stops arranging. "Just . . . set it on the floor. I'll pack the freezer."

He sets the box down and heads up the stairs two at a time. "There's another box," he calls over his shoulder.

"I should hope so," Kendall says. "Or else it's a really small cow. One of them mini cows." Nobody hears her.

A moment later Jacián is back. He flips his sunglasses to rest on top of his head, and he starts unpacking the box. Kendall blocks him from putting anything away. "It's okay, really. I got it."

"My grandfather said I'm supposed to do this," he says. "It's part of the Hector Farms' service." His voice turns sarcastic at the end, and Kendall remembers her conversation with Hector.

"It's really not necessary." Kendall is in the organizing groove, and she wants it done just right.

"You're doing it wrong, anyway. Put all the steaks together, hamburger together, roasts together. Not by size and shape but by category, or you'll never know how much of one item you have left."

Kendall stops cold, stands up straight, and glares at him. She puts one hand on her hip and holds a two-pound package of frozen hamburger in the other. "Go force your condescending man-logic on the next house. You can go now."

He glares back and doesn't leave. He works his jaw, like he wants to say something.

Kendall's mind flashes to Tiffany Quinn. She glances at the freezer, picturing it full of chopped-up abducted girls, and then looks back at Jacián, whose black eyes are on fire now. A wave of irrational fear moves through her chest, and she tries not to show it on her face. She's down in the cellar with a kidnapper, nobody else home. "Go away. Please."

Jacián's eyes narrow, then soften. "Fine." He steps back, turns sharply, and walks up the stairs. Kendall hears his feet and the click of the front door closing.

She glances over her shoulder nervously as she packs the beef in the freezer. By size and shape. It's the only way she can stand to do it.

She rushes through her shower and gets ready. Waits until almost noon for him to show up. And then she calls Nico's house. Nico's line is busy. Kendall hangs up and calls the home line instead. Mrs. Cruz answers.

"Hey, Mrs. Cruz. Nico there?"

"Kendall! No, haven't seen him up yet this morning. Leave a message?"

"Hmm." Kendall thinks. "We're supposed to go to Bozeman today. Maybe you should wake him up."

"Sure thing. I'll have him call you in a minute."

"Thanks!"

"Bye, hon."

"Bye, Mrs. Cruz."

Kendall hangs up and flips on the TV. The news anchor talks about that sixteen-year-old serial killer in Brazil again—the girl who killed twelve people. Wow. Just wait until she tells Nico. Makes Jacián the teenage kidnapper look just a little bit lame.

Twenty minutes pass, and Kendall grows concerned that Nico hasn't called. Just when she's about to call him again, the phone rings.

It's Nico's mother.

"Kendall," she says, her voice distressed, "Nico's not home. His bed is made. There's no note."

Kendall's stomach jumps into her throat before she can think rationally. "Is his car gone?"

"Yes."

"Okay. Well, that's good, then, right? He's probably

just out somewhere." Kendall's tongue is thick. She swallows hard. Breathes.

"Yes, that's probably it," Mrs. Cruz says, and then she laughs anxiously.

Kendall whispers, "Maybe he went to Bozeman without me."

EIGHT

They find the car. It's not in Bozeman. It's parked at the school.

And Nico's not there.

After a cursory search through the town and all around the school grounds, Nico's parents start contacting everybody they can think of, asking if they've seen him.

There is no sign of Nico Cruz.

Nico's car engine is cold, and according to Sheriff Greenwood, there are no clues inside. Not in the car, or in the school. Still, they tape off everything as a precaution. After what happened with Tiffany Quinn, it's never too soon to suspect a missing person. Everybody's on edge.

* * *

When Kendall hears the news about the car, she runs the mile from her house to the school. The car looks so lonely sitting there, surrounded by onlookers. Air crushes her chest. She sinks to her knees, can't catch her breath. People start crowding around her to see the car, the school . . . as if there is something to see. But there's nothing. Just a car, a building. Yellow tape.

"He could be fine," someone says. "Maybe we're all overreacting. He's practically a grown man. Maybe he's out for a hike."

"Maybe he's hunting back in the woods."

"Maybe his car ran out of gas and he pulled in here."

"Yes, let's not jump to conclusions."

But the other whispers are there too, growing louder. "Another one. What's happening to our safe little town? All the children are disappearing."

Kendall tries, fails to tune them all out.

It's all she can do to just breathe. And count.

Count breaths: thirty-six. Count stones in the dirt: more than fifty. Count people saying stupid things: all of them.

Count all the days she's known him: infinity.

Maybe he'll be back before she's done counting.

Maybe not.

* * *

The buzzing noise of the people grows louder and louder, and Kendall can't think. She can't count with so much distraction. She stands up and shoves through the crowd, screaming, "Shut up! Shut up! Shut up! All of you just shut up!" Tears blur everything.

Someone grabs her sleeve. Blindly she whips her arm away and runs, runs like hell. Runs almost all the way home, until her feet can't keep up with her and she plunges forward, down onto the gravel, shredding her palms and knees. And then she just lies there as a huge splash of hurt rips through her body, and she's so grateful for the pain, because she can feel it. It lets something else loose. She sobs. There in the gravel on the side of the road in front of Nico's farm, she sobs, under the old rusty mailbox where she used to put notes for him, grasshoppers and bees fly and buzz around her in a panic.

It's not long before she hears feet crunching on the gravel. When the sound stops next to her, she lifts her head and looks up, squinting into the sun. Her lip starts quivering again. "Mom," she says.

"I couldn't run quite as fast as you," she says, "but at least you ran in the right direction."

Kendall slowly pushes herself up to her feet. Tries to wipe the gravel out of her hands and knees, but some of it's stuck hard. She starts crying again and gives up as Mrs. Fletcher wraps her arms around the girl.

"Come on inside," Kendall's mom says. "Let's get you cleaned up. Sheriff Greenwood is coming over in a few minutes. He wants to talk to you."

Kendall jerks her head up. "Why?"

"Just to get an idea of who saw him last. Nobody thinks you did anything. They think he left the house late last night."

"Why would he do that?" Kendall limps up the long driveway to their farmhouse. "I think my brain is going to burst," she says. "My OCD is going crazy."

"I know, honey. This is hard. But we've got to stay hopeful, okay? He's a big strong guy. He can take care of himself. We just need to figure out what happened. Find out where he is."

Kendall nods. Inside the house she works on cleaning her wounds. Mrs. Fletcher turns on the news, but there's nothing about Nico yet. Takes a while for word to travel to civilization from way out here.

Sheriff Greenwood arrives, cowboy hat in hand. With him is someone Kendall doesn't recognize.

"Afternoon, Mrs. Fletcher, Kendall. This is Sergeant Dunne from the Montana State Police. He's here to help us find Nico."

"Hello, please sit down," Mrs. Fletcher says, pointing to the dining table. She walks through the great room into the kitchen, gets cups, saucers, and the coffee pot, and pours coffee automatically, as if the two cops come over for coffee every day.

They sit at the dining room table, and Sheriff Greenwood takes out a notepad. "For the sake of time, we're going to get right into the questions here, okay?" He continues without looking up to see the nods. "Now, Kendall, can you describe your relationship with Nico Cruz?"

Kendall is immediately flustered. "What do you mean? We're neighbors, best friends since we were little kids. You know that."

Sergeant Dunne leans in and says, "Are you all dating?"

"Yes, I guess so. I mean, we don't really go out all that much, but yeah . . . sort of."

Sergeant Dunne nods. "So he's your boyfriend?"

"No. I mean . . ." Kendall looks to her mother for help.

"Kendall doesn't like to use that term because it feels too much like a commitment, but yes, for all intents and purposes here, Nico is Kendall's boyfriend." Mrs. Fletcher holds Kendall's hand and squeezes it. She looks at Kendall and says, "Okay?"

Kendall nods. She agrees. She just can't say it.

"Okay," Sheriff Greenwood says. "When did you last see Nico?"

"Yesterday at school. I had to go into town to pick up a few things after school. He went home."

"What things?"

Kendall blushes deeply. "Tampons. Not that it's any of your business."

"Kendall," Mrs. Fletcher says, "they're just trying to figure things out."

"Sorry, miss," Sergeant Dunne says. "So that was at what time?"

"Three thirty-five, I guess."

"You didn't see him after that?"

"No."

"Did you talk with him last night? E-mail, phone?"

"He calls me most nights around eleven."

"Did he call last night?"

Kendall hesitates, trying to remember. "Actually, I don't know. I fell asleep on the couch down here watching TV. Mom?"

"I didn't hear your phone ring," Mrs. Fletcher says. She turns to the men. "Kendall has her own phone line in her bedroom. It didn't ring down here, as far as I know, but Dad and I were asleep by ten."

"You go to bed early on a Friday night," the sergeant says lightly.

Mrs. Fletcher looks at him sharply. "We live on a farm. Day begins at five a.m., sir. We don't pause for the weekends."

Sergeant Dunne nods. "Yes, ma'am." He turns back to Kendall. "So you don't think he called?"

"I *don't know* if he called. I can't hear my phone ring down here."

Dunne looks at Greenwood. "I'll have them check phone records. Please write your phone number here, Miss Fletcher. Nico's, too, please."

"Didn't Mr. and Mrs. Cruz already give you Nico's number?" Mrs. Fletcher asks.

"Ma'am, there could be more than one number. Teenagers hide things from their parents all the time. Don't they, Kendall?" He glances at her.

She glares back at him. "I don't."

Mrs. Fletcher pours more coffee.

"All righty, Kendall," Sheriff Greenwood says. "How has Nico been acting lately? The same as always, or different? Anything unusual that springs to mind?"

Kendall swallows hard. She doesn't like Sergeant Dunne. Doesn't want to say anything that might make Nico look bad. But she knows she has to tell the truth. "He's been acting preoccupied the last few days." Her voice catches a little, but she controls it. "We were supposed to go to Bozeman today to look at Montana State. He wants to be a nurse. So I think he had that on his mind."

Sheriff Greenwood writes for a moment. "What else do you think could have made him act preoccupied? Anything?"

Kendall thinks hard. Shakes her head. "Nothing I can think of."

"Were you two having relationship problems?"

"No. I mean, I asked him if he was acting weird because of me, and he said no, he loved me just like always." Kendall chokes on a deep sob that comes from her gut. Mrs. Fletcher puts her arm around Kendall. She's crying too now. The bad thoughts start going in Kendall's head again. Stuff she can't control. Could Jacián have done something to Nico, too?

Sheriff Greenwood writes a few more things, and then closes his notebook. "Okay. That's it for now."

Kendall looks up. "Are you going to question Jacián Obregon?"

Mrs. Fletcher turns sharply toward Kendall, surprised.

Sheriff Greenwood shakes his head firmly and says with an edge in his voice, as if he's said it ten times before, "Jacián Obregon is not a suspect here or in Tiffany Quinn's case. Do you have reason to think he should be? Real reason, I mean, not just rumors?"

Kendall opens her mouth, and then she closes it again. And then says, "No, sir."

"Good. Then, let's leave him out of it. He's been through enough."

Kendall stares at the sheriff. "I'm sorry," she says after a moment.

He nods and smiles sympathetically, and suddenly he's Eli's dad again. "No harm done." He stands up, and Sergeant Dunne follows. "We're going to do everything we can to find him."

"Are we going to do a massive search thing, like with Tiffany?" It strikes Kendall that a search could turn up absolutely nothing, just like last time. She can't let herself believe it.

"It's being planned right now, and the first responder teams are already out there, just in case. You should get a call this evening with instructions for an organized search first thing tomorrow. Hopefully we'll find he's just out hiking in the foothills or something and it won't be necessary."

"Thank you," Kendall says. Mrs. Fletcher walks them to the door. Kendall lowers her head to the table. Numb. She knows he's not hiking. He would never do that alone. Not without her.

Just then, Sergeant Dunne pops his head back in. "By the way, Kendall, what was the relationship between Nico and Tiffany Quinn? Did they know each other?"

Kendall lifts her head and looks at Sergeant Dunne.

She narrows her eyes. "Of course. Have you seen the size of this town? Everybody knows everybody."

He smiles disarmingly. "Did they ever do anything together? You know . . . maybe there was something going on between them." He pauses. "It's an awfully strange coincidence, two kids from a town this small."

Kendall slowly sits up. "No," she says. "No, there was nothing *going on* between them. She was just a kid."

"At the time of her disappearance, she was fifteen. Nico was seventeen." He stops, as if that explains something. "Were you and Nico dating then?"

Kendall speaks through gritted teeth. "Yes. Sort of."

"Did he ever take you to any secret places, in the mountains or the woods, to get away from everybody? Maybe to be alone, have sex?"

"No!" she says, flustered. "We aren't that serious. We aren't . . . sexually active."

"Oh, right. You said that you didn't want a commitment in the relationship. Were you two free to see others, then?"

Kendall shakes her head, trying to grasp what he's really saying, feeling like she's in an episode of *Law & Order: SVU*. "He wasn't seeing her. I know he wasn't. Okay?"

Sergeant Dunne is quiet for a moment, looking at Kendall. And then he says in a low voice, "Well, maybe he is now."

Mrs. Fletcher stands quickly as Kendall shoves her

chair back and gets up. It makes an awful scraping sound on the wooden floor. Her hands are trembling. "What are you saying?"

"We're just covering all our bases. Running through all the scenarios." His cliché-laden monotone is deeply annoying.

"Why would he do anything to her? If they wanted to be together, nobody was stopping them!"

Sergeant Dunne tilts his head. "Maybe he got a little frustrated with your noncommitment and did something he was ashamed of. I don't know. You tell me."

"Well, you're wrong!" Kendall's voice breaks.

Mrs. Fletcher steps in, her voice clear and firm. "Sergeant, is there anything else?"

Sergeant Dunne doesn't take his eyes off Kendall, though his gaze softens a bit. For a moment he doesn't move. And then he says, "No, ma'am, that's it for today." He nods once and steps back outside. "Let us know if you think of anything else that might help us find your friend," he says to Kendall.

Kendall flees the kitchen and runs upstairs to her room.

Falls apart. Sobbing. So lost in this situation, she cannot handle it. Her brain can't handle it.

All she can do is try. Try to stop picturing Nico and Tiffany in some secret mountain hideout having sex together.

WE

Panting in the depths of a lightless night, We sigh in collective. You made your way through, found your new home nestled in the ground. Your sacrifice has been received. Another trapped soul set free.

Our remaining souls beg, bloodthirsty now. Soul-thirsty. Together, imprisoned inside wood and metal, We wait again and scratch anew.

Touch me.

NINE

By early morning the national news networks pick it up. This small-town teen runaway story is no longer worthy of only a tiny blip on the radar of Bozeman TV. Within twenty-four hours it has become the unfortunate American horror sensation of the week. Nico's face is splashed all over TV, and Tiffany Quinn's entire history is resurrected and replayed along with Nico's history. It's not long before reporters try to connect the two in sinister ways, just like Sergeant Dunne did yesterday with Kendall. Did Nico "make Tiffany disappear" and now has disappeared himself? Where could they be? What is the dark side of Nico Cruz?

Oh, yes, it's all speculation. The reporters admit it.

But you can tell they believe it.

* * *

Mr. Fletcher turns the TV off. Kendall stares at the blank screen, her hair disheveled, eyes red.

"Kendall," he says. He puts his hand on her arm.

She doesn't move.

"Honey."

Kendall just shakes her head. Whispers, her throat sore from crying, "I can't believe this is happening."

Her father stands up, pulls her to her feet. Hugs her close and whispers, "Come on, pumpkin."

Kendall nods, her cheek against his shoulder. When she pulls away, she sees the shine in his eyes.

He looks away. "Let's go find him."

There are helicopters. News teams are arriving, setting up camp in front of the Feed and Seed shop and inside the farmers' market.

More police mill around than Kendall's ever seen before in one place. Many people drive or walk to the town center, but several come on four-wheelers for the sake of faster off-road searching. Marlena and Jacián are among them. Kendall narrows her eyes.

Sheriff Greenwood stands on the steps of the restaurant with a bullhorn, and he holds it up, testing it out to get everybody's attention.

Kendall looks around. It's barely dawn on a Sunday

morning, and everybody is here, just like last time. Except for Nico.

Students eye Kendall warily, sympathetically, looking unsure if they should approach her. Most don't. Kendall and her parents walk over to Nico's parents and stand quietly, the moms exchanging hugs. Nothing much to say. Lack of sleep is evident in all their faces, and that says it all. Kendall sees Tiffany Quinn's mother standing in the crowd. She looks old, like she's aged ten years since May. Kendall glances at Nico's parents and wonders what will happen to them.

Sheriff Greenwood speaks, quiets everyone down.

Everything is so horribly familiar, and for Kendall, a thousand times worse.

"Thanks for coming out," Sheriff Greenwood's voice booms. He clears his throat as the crowd grows silent, and he lifts the bullhorn to his lips again. "It seems impossible that we are doing this again. Yet here we are."

He pauses a moment, glancing at a white paper that shakes in his hand in the breeze. "To give you an update, we officially declared Nico Cruz a missing person at around seven p.m. yesterday. We've spoken to a number of people since then, and trained officials have been searching overnight. We've found no sign of him at this point.

"I've decided, after conferring with the other law enforcement who've come down to help us, that we'll run our search much like last time. This time, however, there will be no groups smaller than three, and no child under eighteen will be permitted to travel anywhere alone from now on, until further notice. Not on foot or by car or horseback. That's not just for the search—that's a new Cryer's Cross curfew."

There is a wave of murmuring in the crowd, not just surprise but fear.

"Let me define that further: No child or teenager seventeen and younger shall travel alone in the village limits of Cryer's Cross at any time until further notice. Children thirteen and under must be accompanied by someone over eighteen. Teens fourteen and up will be allowed to move about using a buddy system. You will be assigned school buddies based on where you live, for the sake of convenience." He pauses. "If you do not comply, you will be arrested."

Arrested? Kendall stares at the Sheriff. *School buddies?* The only other teenager who lived in her direction from school was Nico.

There is more murmuring. "Quiet, please," urges the sheriff. "This is very important. We don't want to lose another one of you. Please feel confident that even though I've known most of you teenagers since you were babies, I will not hesitate to arrest you if I see you wandering or driving alone. We don't yet know what we are dealing with here, and we must proceed with appropriate caution rather than foolishness."

He pauses. "Let's start searching. Please find your same groups from spring and wait for instruction. If you are in need of a group, see me. Stay together, return together. Teens, when you return today, see me. I'll have the buddy list ready."

Kendall glances at Mrs. Cruz, who holds tightly to her husband. It sounds like Sheriff Greenwood expects they won't find Nico today, the way he's planning this buddy thing. It feels terrible.

The sheriff lowers the bullhorn, a resolute look on his face. Then he nods, and people disperse into groups on the sides of the streets.

Kendall stays close to her parents at her mother's request. It's kind of comforting, since Kendall is group-less. Last time she searched with Nico.

The tone is somber and way too familiar as the groups get their instructions and set out to comb the most remote part of the valley again. Last time everything was freshly planted. This time the potato fields are plump and green, ripe for harvest, and the leaves on the trees are just start-ing to change colors. Kendall wonders how many days her parents can search when there's so much to do on the farm right now. But she's too tired to ask. All she can do is wearily count steps, and rows, and trees, repeating crazy sentences in her mind as she scans the vegetables and grain, and then goes on to grassy fields and woods. Looking for the body of her best friend. Torn between hoping she finds it and hoping she doesn't.

She doesn't. No one else finds him either.

When they return to town, Sheriff Greenwood is there, talking with Hector, Jacián, and Marlena, and what must be their parents.

Kendall stops. Doesn't want to see Jacián right now. Still doesn't know what to think of him. And certainly doesn't want him to say anything to her about Nico. Fresh tears spring to her eyes as she pictures going to school without Nico there.

"Stop it," she mutters to herself. "He'll be back."

But it feels so much more futile this time. With Tiffany everyone was so hopeful. Now that disappearing seems to have become an epidemic, the hope is gone.

"Dad?" Kendall says. "We have to find him. I want to keep searching. It's not dark yet."

Mr. Fletcher checks his watch. He glances at Mrs. Fletcher.

"I'm in for another round," Mrs. Fletcher says. "Why don't you head back to the farm, Nathan. Kendall and I will go out again with someone else."

Kendall smiles tearfully. "Thanks, Mom." They go out with another group.

After dusk, when Kendall and her mother return, they find Sheriff Greenwood again. Exhausted, Mrs. Fletcher goes into the restaurant to call Kendall's dad to come out and pick them up. Kendall approaches Sheriff Greenwood.

"I need my school buddy assignment," Kendall says. She's so tired she can barely hold back the tears now.

Sheriff Greenwood glances at her and takes his clipboard out. "You're all alone out that direction," he muses.

"No kidding." Kendall can't help it. She's still stinging from yesterday's interrogation, even though the sheriff played the good cop.

He mumbles, "Eli's grouping with the north end. Travis is east, but one of you would have to travel alone to meet up . . . hmm."

Kendall scratches the toe of her boot in the dirt as the sheriff reconfigures his list.

Darkness descends quickly without big-city lights. The stars twinkle. She hears the four-wheelers before she sees them. It's Marlena and Jacián.

"Ah, now there's a thought," Sheriff Greenwood mutters, looking up. "Yes. That'll work." He turns toward them. "You two can swing by for Kendall on school days, right?"

Jacián is silent, and in the dark, Kendall can't gauge his reaction. Marlena pipes up, "Sure. We'd love to." She climbs off and goes over to Kendall. Gives her a swift hug. "I'm really sorry. You must feel horrible," she says softly.

Kendall's throat tightens. She nods. Can't speak.

"We covered miles and miles, made it to the foothills and up beyond Cryer's Pass, along the woods, and back."

"That's awesome," Kendall says, without enthusiasm. Her body aches. She just wants to crawl into bed and forget everything.

"Jacián and I can give you a ride home now if you need one. You look exhausted."

"My dad's coming. Thanks." She's almost asleep on her feet.

At home she checks all the windows and doors in the entire house before falling into bed.

WE

The quiet stretch unsettles, rattles Our aching souls. We roam the floor, bitter, restless, shoving others out of Our way. Searching for new life. And then We grow quiet and return to Our spot. Remembering, hoping.

We save Our energy for another day.

TEN

After a week of chaos the local search for Nico Cruz
ends. They've combed every accessible section of the valley on foot. Every American with a TV has heard about
the strange situation in "quaint" Cryer's Cross, Montana,
where young, innocent Tiffany disappeared in spring,
and sinister, older bad boy Nico disappeared only months
later . . . probably because he killed her. Or brainwashed
her into hiding out for three months so they could fool
people into thinking their disappearances were unrelated.

Never mind the quiet girlfriend, Kendall. She keeps
her head down and doesn't talk to the reporters. Does she
know something? Speculation ad infinitum.

Kendall can't stand it.

Every morning Kendall wakes up and remembers. And every evening at eleven her phone doesn't ring. More than once she thinks about calling Nico's number just because it feels like a connection, but she doesn't want to startle his family, make them remember, force them to relive their personal horror any more times than they already do.

Over the course of the week Kendall goes from shock to mourning to frustration and fury. The news crews are bored, tired of having only one restaurant to eat in and no fast food within thirty miles. Tired of the loyal, tight-lipped people. They try to get a fresh angle, but the people of Cryer's Cross are a quiet, protective group. Even Jacián just gives them a look and walks away when they yell out questions to him.

Kendall sits on the restaurant steps, waiting for her mother to stop chatting inside the drugstore. She pushes her hair off her forehead. It falls back again when she stares down at her hands. Behind her, old Mr. Greenwood and Hector Morales sit in their chairs, not talking. As usual.

Jacián comes toward them. "*Abuelo*," he says sharply. "Are you coming now with me?" Kendall notices that he takes on a hint of an accent when he speaks to his grandfather.

Jacián ignores Kendall, walks right past her up the steps.

Hector looks up and says something to Jacián in Spanish. Jacián replies in Spanish and then turns, jogs down the steps and to his four-wheeler. He heads off alone.

Kendall turns and squints at Hector. "Jacián isn't supposed to be going off alone, you know. He could get arrested."

Hector smiles, but he looks worried. "He's okay. He's already eighteen, and stubborn. What can I say? Sheriff says he's legal to go alone, just stupid. It's nice of you to worry about him, though."

"I'm not worried about him," Kendall says crossly. How can she explain it? The rule-follower in her can't help but say something.

"I'm sorry, Miss Kendall. Truly. About the Cruz boy. I know he was your beau."

Kendall stares at the dirt between the steps. "He's not dead," she says. "He still is my . . . my beau." She cringes at the old-fashioned word. It's odd how the longer Nico is gone, the easier it is to call him her boyfriend.

Hector is quiet. Kendall glances at him to make sure he's not mad at her tone, and he assures her with a sympathetic smile.

"Where's Marlena?" she asks. "Did she search today?"

"She took a fall last night, so she's been down all day. She hit a rut that was hidden by brush and she flipped off her four-wheeler. She got a little too cocky with it, going too fast." He says it softly, his hand shielding his mouth. "Don't let the news crews hear of it."

"Oh, no," Kendall says. She pulls herself out of her

own misery for a moment. "Is she okay?" She remembers suddenly that tonight would have been the first soccer game of the season, but Coach canceled because of Nico.

"She broke her leg and dislocated her shoulder," he says. "She'll be okay."

Kendall's eyes bug out. "Oh my God. That's terrible!" Her fingers flutter up to her throat. "I can't believe this. I'm so sorry, Hector. I didn't know. Is there anything I can do?"

He tilts his head and glances at old Mr. Greenwood. "As I always say, people in tough times need tough friends. Right, friend?"

Mr. Greenwood grunts.

Finally Kendall's mother emerges from the drugstore. She grabs Hector's hand and squeezes it. "I just heard about poor Marlena inside," she whispers. "So sorry to hear it. I'll drop Kendall by to visit tonight."

Hector raises an eyebrow at Kendall, as if to say, *See? This is how it's done*, but all he says is, "Yes, ma'am. She'll appreciate that."

As Mrs. Fletcher and Kendall walk home, the news trucks come roaring past on their way out of Cryer's Cross, leaving a trail of dust. For them the story is over.

ELEVEN

Kendall sits in silence as Mrs. Fletcher drives her to Hector's ranch. She's tired. Not quite ready for life to resume.

"Call me when you're ready to be picked up."

"Okay," Kendall says with a sigh. "How about now?"

"It'll be good for you to think about someone else for a bit," Mrs. Fletcher says carefully. "Help you cope."

Kendall doesn't have any tears left. She's too weary to voice what she and her mother both know—that Nico is probably inexplicably gone forever, just like Tiffany, and life has to go on. In a farming town it is a simple fact of survival. The produce, the animals—no one can make living things pause in their growing. Not one human event can make the potatoes wait. When they are ready, they are ready.

* * *

Kendall pauses at the front door of Hector's house as her mother drives back down the long driveway. Jacián is in the grassy yard between the house and a corral. A floodlight shines on a soccer goal. Half a dozen soccer balls are scattered over the grass and around the net, and Jacián dribbles one slowly, then fakes left and spins around an invisible opponent. He passes the ball to himself and sprints to the goal, smashing the ball into the net at a sharp angle.

He moves like a dancer.

He reaches down to pick up a ball and sees Kendall standing there. They stare at each other for a moment. Then Kendall breaks the stare and knocks on the door.

Mr. Obregon lets Kendall in. He and Mrs. Obregon greet her warmly and thank her for coming. They usher her through the house to the family room, where Marlena rests on the sofa, right leg in a cast that reaches to midthigh. Her left shoulder is immobilized in a sling. Hector sits nearby in an old rocking chair. Marlena's eyes are closed, but she stirs when Kendall comes in.

"Hey," she says with a sleepy smile. A single crutch lies on the floor next to her.

"Hey," Kendall says, taking it all in. "Wow. Did they keep you at the hospital overnight? This looks . . . really serious."

Marlena grins. "Yeah, but it's not as bad as it looks. The fracture's nice and small—cast on for four weeks, maybe six.

My foot itches like crazy, though. The shoulder—I dislocated it before once in a soccer tournament back in Tucson. This time it popped right back in. Swelling's going down already. Just hurt like a futhermucker for a few minutes."

"Marlena," Hector says. He narrows his eyes and shakes his head slightly, but Hector couldn't look mean if he tried.

"Sorry, *Abuelo*. It's the painkillers." Marlena looks guilty.

Hector chuckles. "What makes you do it the rest of the time, hmm? You must be always on the painkillers."

"It wasn't even a real swear!"

"It is the intent, not the word, that makes something harsh," Hector says. "So yes, I agree. In this case you are off the hook." He turns to Kendall and reaches out. "How are you this evening, Miss Kendall?"

Kendall walks over to him and takes his hand for a minute. "I'm okay," she says with a shrug. "At least I'm not in pain like Marlena." *Or like Nico. He might be in pain too, if he's even alive.* She glances out the picture window behind Hector to where Jacián continues to work soccer plays. He nails the goalpost, and the ball ricochets out. Kendall sees Jacián yell his frustration, but she can't hear him. She nods out the window. "Does he do that a lot?"

"Every evening with Marlena," Hector says. "It's his dream to play professional."

Marlena eases to a sitting position and follows Kendall's gaze. "He looks so alone out there. He's worried."

"About what?" Kendall asks.

"The team."

"Yeah," Kendall says. "Me too. Losing . . . losing Nico. . . ." She turns abruptly to look at Marlena. "Oh, crap. And you. Der. I . . . ." She thinks for a minute, and then her lips part as she realizes. They are down to six players. Their already too small team is now no team at all.

Marlena presses her lips together and looks like she's going to cry. "I heard Jacián on the phone with Coach tonight after dinner. He was trying not to yell. Then he went storming out there. It's been hours." Her voice quivers. "I feel so bad."

"Well, there's no rule that says we can't play," Kendall says, but her heart sinks. "Just common sense. Eight was already too tight. Six . . ." She trails off. She was counting on soccer to bring her out of her misery. If she can't dance or act, playing soccer is her savior. It's the only other thing that can occupy her mind enough to stop the whirling in her brain. "Maybe there's a freshman we can coerce, just to get our numbers," she says, but she already knows that Coach has begged every eligible kid in school just to get the eight they have—or had, as of a week ago.

"You know there's not," Marlena says, miserable. "Coach is tapped out."

They sit together in silence, mourning for different reasons.

After a minute Marlena says, "How are Nico's parents?"

"In front of me they seem fine. Like they're really trying to be upbeat for my sake. My mom says they're having a terrible time, though. He's their youngest kid and the only one left here. Everybody else moved away."

"That's so sad," Marlena says.

Neither of them really knows what to say.

Hector interrupts the silence. "Maybe you can tell us something about Nico," he says. "Stories always help. Tell Marlena about when you were younger."

Kendall sighs, but humors the older man. "Okay. . . ." She thinks for a minute. "Well, so we've been neighbors since I was born. Nico is two months older than me. We grew up together, rode bikes or walked to each other's house every day. Both of us have farms, and our houses are set really far back from the road, like yours here. Riding my bike to Nico's felt like this really long journey, so I always had to pack a lunch, right?" She smiles a little at the memory. "And then I always felt bad so I packed a lunch for Nico, too, and then I'd ride down the driveway on my bike and stop at the road, looking both ways like fifty times, even though there's hardly any traffic down our road, and I'd get up the nerve and fly across the street and make my way to Nico's, maybe stop and try to catch a grasshopper or whatever. And by the time I got all the way up to his house, I'd be all ready to have my lunch because it felt like a lot of work, but Nico always made me wait. He'd come out and we'd go ride around the tractor trails all through his property, all along the perimeter of their land. Their property backs up to a neighbor who doesn't live there anymore—an old man who died a few years ago, Mr. Prins. Remember him, Hector?"

"Oh, yes. He was a cranky old deaf man. Didn't have a kind word for anybody at the end. I knew him since I was a teenager," Hector says. "He wasn't always so mean, but sometimes things happen that change a person." His eyes cloud.

"Yes, well, I was scared to death of him. But Nico was totally fascinated. He couldn't stay away. He tormented that man and dragged me into it with him. Mr. Prins would be hoeing his garden and we'd stand right behind the property line, as if it somehow protected us, and scream at the top of our lungs, trying to get him to look at us, ready to run like heck if he ever looked up. But he never did."

"I thought he was deaf," Marlena says.

"He was," Kendall says. "Nico figured he was faking it."

"When did you eat your lunch?"

Kendall smiles. "There's a big oak tree in the back corner of their farm. His older sister and brothers built a tree house in it and left it once they grew up. We'd go up there and eat lunch and play all day. He didn't mind playing house with me, or acting in all the dumb little plays I always wrote. It was like we were meant to be together forever."

Marlena looks like she's about to cry again.

"I'm so sorry," she says.

Kendall takes a deep breath, lets it out, and smiles shakily. She leans forward in her chair, puts her chin in her hands. "What am I going to do without him? He's my best friend. It's like half of my soul was ripped out."

Hector quietly eases out of his chair and leaves the girls to talk.

Almost as if Marlena turned a switch, Kendall finds herself spilling everything—her fears, her sadness. How upsetting it was when people insinuated that Nico had something to do with Tiffany's disappearance. She even tells Marlena about her own secret problem. Her obsessive-compulsive disorder, and how this stress is making it harder than ever for her brain to settle down. How she's hoping so much for soccer to help her cope, but now there's that worry too. How this buddy system thing is going to ruin everything. She can't even go for a run when she wants to. And how scared she is, wondering who's next to disappear.

It's after nine when Mrs. Fletcher returns for Kendall. She comes in for a minute, carrying a plastic container of something, and sets it on the counter. Says a quick sympathetic hello to Marlena and makes small talk with Marlena's parents in the kitchen. Kendall, feeling a little vulnerable, gives Marlena a gentle hug good-bye and goes outside, where Hector stands, leaning against the railing of the big wraparound porch, watching Jacián.

"Thanks, Hector," she says, "for making me talk about Nico. That really made me feel better."

Hector nods and smiles. "It always hurts, but it helps, too," he says. "I'm glad you're not so stubborn, like some."

Kendall watches Jacián. He's moving more slowly now. She can only imagine how exhausted he must be. When he slips on dewy grass, he flops to the ground and lies there on his back, chest heaving. "I guess maybe we all have different ways of working things out," she says. "Sometimes they even make sense."

Hector squeezes her hand. "Thank you for coming. Will we see you again tomorrow, then? Marlena won't be in school for a couple days. Not until she can get around on one crutch, or until her shoulder is well enough to handle a second one."

Kendall nods. "Sure, I'll be glad to come by. Maybe I can just. . . ." She pauses as she realizes that it'll be just her and Jacián tomorrow for their first day back.

"Come home with Jacián after soccer, maybe?"

Mrs. Fletcher comes out and closes the door behind her. "Ready, Kendall?"

Kendall squeezes Hector's arm. "Maybe. We'll see." She turns to her mother. "Yep. Ready."

They wave good-bye, and are home four minutes later. Nico's driveway looks dark and lonely.

TWELVE

She doesn't want to get up today.

Everything is about to be very different.

She thinks about faking sick, but she knows her mother will just force her out of bed. "I highly regret this day in advance," she says to the ceiling. Finally she hoists herself out of bed and gets ready for school. She halfheartedly packs her soccer clothes and wonders if she's actually already played the last game of her high school career.

When Jacián pulls up in one of Hector's ranch trucks, Kendall shoves the rest of her toast into her mouth. She chews quickly and swallows, grabs her stuff—then sets it all down again because her OCD won't let her leave the house without brushing her teeth. Jacián comes to the door and knocks.

She spits out the toothpaste, rinses her mouth, and wipes it dry, then grabs her books and runs to the door. He's standing in her way.

"Hi," she says.

He nods curtly. "Ready?"

"Yeah."

He strides over to the pickup and opens her door for her. Stands there impatiently as she stares him down, Kendall wondering what his possible motive could be.

"You don't need to do that," Kendall says. "I can handle getting a door myself."

"My grandfather will ask you if I opened the door for you." He goes to the driver's side. "I'm just trying to make the old man happy."

"I'll tell him yes. From now on."

"Fine."

He starts the truck and turns around in the driveway, navigating the bumps carefully. Kendall glances at him and slumps against her door, hugging her book bag. She stares out the window as he turns onto the gravel road. She looks over her family's farm, and she hates this day. Hates everything about it. She sees her father up on the big combine as Jacián's truck picks up speed. Her father doesn't see her. He's trying desperately to catch up for all the time he spent searching for Nico, she knows. She won't see much of him until after harvest is over.

They drive in silence. Jacián pulls into the dirt parking area next to the school building. He parks and turns off the ignition and sits there. Kendall looks at him, and then back at her lap.

"You talked to Coach," she says.

He nods. Doesn't look at her.

"What did he say about the team?"

He pulls the keys from the ignition. Opens his door. "He said he'll let us know what's going to happen at practice today." He clears his throat and gets out of the truck. Heads for the door to the school and goes inside.

Kendall gets out too and shuts the door. Watches the students coming to school in groups now. And then she feels her chest tighten. She remembers all of her rituals—the wastebasket, the markers, the curtains, straightening the desks. Her heart drops and she hurries inside, sees that some of the students are already sitting down. Fear stabs through her. This can't happen.

Everything is thrown off, and she can't let anybody see how weird she is. Anxiously she glances at the wastebasket and nudges it with her foot until it's properly turned. The markers are askew so she saunters over to them as if she's going to draw a silly picture on the white board like some of the other students do. Instead she bumps the tray and knocks them onto the floor. She picks them up again and puts them in their proper order. And then she goes over to the windows where other students mingle, whispering about how weird it is to be back after what happened, again. She tugs at the curtains that she can reach and lines them up, pretending like she's looking for someone. One window remains blocked, people standing in her way. She bites her lip anxiously, trying to maneuver a path, but finally she just gives up and leaves it. She hurries over to the senior section, trying to straighten a few desks as she goes, and feeling an overwhelming failure. She knows it's not going to be right. She doesn't notice Jacián watching her, a look of mild curiosity on his face.

She slips into her desk next to Jacián and taps her fingers anxiously, unable to do anything about it. It's going to bother her all day, she knows. Maybe at lunch she can take care of things.

And then, when she sets her backpack on the floor, she turns to her right, like she's done every day for twelve years. To talk to Nico.

And no one is there. His desk is empty.

Every bad thing comes rushing at her. Every emotion—surprise, grief, fear, anger. She gasps a little as she experiences the moment she's been dreading for days now. And then she feels the rush of a sob coming so fast and hard she can't stop it.

"Fuuuck," she gasps. She buries her head in her arms on her desk and fights it for as long as she can. She doesn't want to cry anymore. Not here, especially not now. Not in front of everybody. Because Kendall's supposed to be strong. She's tough. She's grown up with boys surrounding her. She played and got hurt with them on the playground, and she didn't cry then. She broke her nose playing dodgeball in seventh grade when Eli Greenwood winged one at her face from six feet away, and she didn't cry then—not for real, just the stinging tears that happen automatically when your nose gets hit. And she even broke her arm when she jumped off the bag swing at its highest point, at the river with Nico where he liked to fish with his dad. Totally missed the water, landed on the bank. It was a drought summer that year.

She didn't cry then, either, but Nico carried her home, the bone just barely piercing through the skin of her forearm, and even though she said she didn't want him to carry her, she really was a little bit too faint over seeing her own bone to fight it too hard.

That was the first day he kissed her.

And now here she is, bawling in front of all the boys she grew up with.

Almost all, that is. The most important one is missing.

That makes her cry harder.

After a minute she feels a hand squeezing her shoulder. Hears a voice by her ear. "It's okay, Kendall." It's Eli

Greenwood's voice. Kendall takes a deep, shuddering breath and tries again to contain her sorrow. She lifts her head. Eli is crying too.

She rummages for a tissue in her backpack. "Sorry, guys," she says. "Stupid me. God." She feels embarrassed. "Where's a tissue when you need it, huh?" She knows her nose must be bright red. She sniffs hard.

"Dude, it's cool," Travis says from behind her. Even Brandon isn't saying anything. She glances at him, and he looks miserable.

They've all been affected. For the seniors this hit feels so much more personal than Tiffany Quinn. Kendall thinks maybe she knows a little better how Tiffany's closest friends must have felt. She looks over to the sophomore section and catches the eye of Tiffany's best friend, Jocelyn. The girl gives Kendall a sympathetic smile, and Kendall smiles gratefully in return.

Jacián, quiet all this time, but watching, points a finger toward the front of the classroom, where Ms. Hinkler stands, trying to get the students' attention. "You still need a tissue?" he asks gruffly. "I'll get you one."

"No, I'm okay," Kendall says. "Thanks."

Jacián nods as Eli goes back to his seat. Everyone settles in to try to concentrate.

For most of them the only way to get through it is by moving on.

THIRTEEN

Somehow she makes it through to lunch, when she gets a chance to straighten the curtain and the desks. She can't stand to go outside to eat lunch in their spot. She can hardly stand to look at Nico's desk. It's so empty. So cold.

By afternoon she can no longer concentrate at all, and even Ms. Hinkler is giving her a free pass indefinitely to lay her head down and just try to get through it.

When school is over, there's nothing Kendall wants more than to play some soccer. Get the whirlwind out of her head. Work out the grief and the anxiety. Think about something else for a change.

She suits up in the locker room, alone again without Marlena, and makes a little wish that Coach has found more players to join the team before they miss another game. Tomorrow is the next one scheduled in Bozeman. She runs out to the field and starts warming up. Counting to thirty for every stretch, counting her steps as she jogs in place. Slowly the others join her. She counts them, just to make sure.

Four seniors. One freshman. Only one sophomore now. Six.

Coach is late, and the team falls into a three-on-three scrimmage naturally, anxiously. Kendall feels naked without Nico there. They had so many plays together. So much nonverbal communication. Years of it. There's no quick fix when you're missing that.

Jacián is also looking a little bit lost for plays without Marlena. The two end up on the same team with Brandon, and they fail miserably, like it's their first game ever.

They scrimmage for twenty painful minutes before Coach shows up. When he strides onto the field, everybody comes to a standstill. He waves them all in.

"Guys," he says. Kendall notices the wrinkles by his eyes for the first time. He looks tired. He waits for everybody to quiet, glancing at his clipboard, fingering the whistle around his neck.

"Hey, guys, gather up. It's good to see you again." He gives a grim smile. "Wish it were under better circumstances. We've lost two of our best at the moment. Update, Jacián?"

"She had a rough night, but she's tough." Jacián's dark skin gleams with sweat in the afternoon sun. "Doc says she won't play this season at all, though." He looks down. "Sorry, guys. She feels bad."

Kendall looks at the grass.

"And you've all figured out by now that we're down to six. Last year we played with nine and it was tough. This year with eight would have been already approaching impossible. It's different with one game, but game after game for a whole season . . ." Coach pauses. He shakes his head as if he doesn't want to say what he has to say next.

"I made a dozen phone calls last night, people. And I don't have a single possibility for new players. Not one. Not even one who hedged or wavered on a maybe. We've squeezed a third of our high school for our soccer sports program. That's a ton more, percentage wise, than most other schools nationwide. We're maxed out." He pauses. Sighs. "We're done, guys. I'm sorry. This is the end of the road for us."

The whole team stares at the ground, nobody daring to look up.

"To you seniors who played your last high school game as juniors," Coach says, "I'm especially sorry. This isn't the way to end a career."

He glances at Jacián and around the group. "Some of you have a lot of talent and have a chance of playing on a college team. I hope you give it a shot. Keep practicing on your own. Don't give up."

Coach pulls his baseball cap from his head, smoothes his cropped hair back, and replaces the cap. "That's it. I'm sorry. We did the best we could. I'll be on the grounds for a bit if anybody wants to talk further." He stands for a minute, almost unsure, and then he turns and walks back toward the school building.

The team stands in silent shock, realizing the season's over, watching their coach walk away for the last time. For some of them their soccer career is over. It's hard to swallow that.

A moment later Jacián walks away, not following the coach but going toward the locker room. Kendall watches as he enters, and then exits again with his backpack and his school clothes rolled up under his arm. He walks to the truck.

"Wait," Kendall says under her breath. He's her only ride if she doesn't want to get arrested. What a crazy messed-up world.

She runs to the girls' locker room and grabs her things. Says a little word of good-bye. This is it for her.

So many good things ending.

She jogs back out, and when she sees that Jacián is still sitting in the truck waiting for her, she slows to a walk. Gets into the truck. They both sit there. Jacián's face is full of rage, but he doesn't speak.

"Can you take me to your house, please?" she says in a dull voice. "I told your grandfather I'd come by today to see Marlena."

Jacián doesn't acknowledge her. A minute later he starts up the truck and peels out of the dirt lot onto the road, going way too fast. The truck fishtails on the loose gravel. Kendall closes her eyes and grips the door's armrest. They hit rocket speed before he bottoms out in a few potholes and eases off the gas.

Out of the blue he slams his fist onto the steering wheel. "Fuck!" he yells at the top of his voice.

Kendall startles and slides closer to her door once again.

He slows the truck as he pulls into the ranch's driveway, and takes a deep breath.

She glances at him. His face is even now. He drives carefully, deliberately.

"I'd appreciate it if you didn't mention that," he says darkly. "The parentals don't really give a shit that they've wrecked my life."

Kendall regards him. "You know, maybe you should get some help with that. Anger management is a good idea," she says.

He laughs bitterly. "You think? Now, where would I go for that? The general store, or maybe the Feed and Seed?"

Kendall ignores him. Looks out her window as Hector's house comes into view. Says quietly, "Why do you have to be such a jerk?"

He pulls the truck into the big barn and doesn't reply. He goes immediately to the corner of the barn and grabs a mesh net full of soccer balls. Heads out to the makeshift soccer field, not looking back.

Kendall goes to the house and knocks on the door.

Hector opens it wide. "Hello, Miss Kendall! How nice of you to come by again."

Kendall smiles. "Nice of you to invite me," she says.

"I am happy to say that Marlena is taking a nap right now. She needs it. But I think you should feel comfortable out here playing soccer, no?"

Kendall looks at him, standing there with his innocent smile. She slumps her shoulders and drops her backpack to the porch. "Seriously, Hector?" Her voice is strained.

"You should call your mother first to let her know you are here, of course." He steps into the kitchen and returns a moment later with the phone.

Kendall sighs. "Maybe she should just come and pick me up."

"Oh, please, no! Marlena has been looking forward to your visit all day. She thought you might be coming later, after soccer practice."

"Yeah, well, there is no soccer practice anymore."

Hector's face falls. "Ah, I'm sorry to hear that. It is a shame for you and for Jacián. Marlena feels responsible."

"It's not her fault," Kendall says automatically. She dials her house and leaves a message saying she's at Hector's. Indefinitely. "You can pick me up anytime if you need me," she says. "See you soon." Trying not to sound desperate.

Hector takes the phone from her and shoos her in the direction of the yard, where Jacián is warming up all over again. "I am going into town to sit with my friend for a bit," he calls out. "Just let yourself in later."

Kendall sighs and goes down the porch steps. "Okay," she says, not wanting to be here. Wishing she could just go hang out with Nico and have everything be okay again.

She walks toward Jacián, waiting for him to reject her. Just what she needs today. Some pompous jerk to tell her to go away. Stupid Hector. He needs to back off.

Jacián sees her coming and doesn't stop stretching. Kendall walks up to him and stands there, awkwardly.

"Yes?" he asks finally.

"Marlena's taking a nap. Hector's going to town."

Jacián squints up at her. "What are you, the butler?"

Kendall rolls her eyes. "Mind if I play? While I wait for Marlena, I mean?"

He lifts himself up to his feet and messes with the net

bag, opening the cinch and letting the balls loose. "It's a big yard." He passes one to her and then dribbles another one up and down the stretch of grass, warming up.

Kendall pulls a ponytail holder from her pocket and whips her hair back into it. She moves out of Jacián's way and warms up too, as if they are at soccer practice. They work individually.

It's not long before Kendall's in the zone. The constant whirring of her thoughts quiets, softens. She counts her steps to one hundred, and then she can stop and really concentrate on the ball. She loves the way it moves over the grass, like a hand on bare skin, seeking out all the nuances. She feels her muscles praise her for the stretch, feels the sweat break out on her forehead. Feels her breath paint a path in front of her.

There is nothing else like it in her world. Nothing else like the bliss of her brain shutting down after seven days of constant whirring. Incredible relief.

She ignores Jacián completely, keeping her distance, and then slowly she begins running some of the plays she used to do with Nico, passing instead to herself, running like hell to catch up and slamming the ball into the net. Retrieving it again and taking it all the way down the side yard, then back and forth, like she's running suicides with the ball. Then back again for another play with invisible Nico.

It's funny how the presence of a memory is a comfort here on the field.

By the time Kendall has worked out all her stress, an hour has passed. She and Jacián successfully avoid each other, though once when his ball gets away from him, Kendall plants it back at his feet, and he acknowledges her with a wave.

Hector would be so proud.

When Kendall is dying of thirst, she calls it quits, hoping Marlena is awake. Jacián's shirt is stuck to his body. Sweat drips off his hair, curled in dark spikes. He's breathing hard as she walks past. She drops her ball by the mesh ball bag. "Thanks," she says.

"All right." He almost smiles.

Impulsively she adds, "You need any water? I'm headed in."

"No, I've got a bottle in my gym bag."

So civil.

Marlena is awake. Kendall grabs a paper towel, wets it, and wipes her face and the back of her neck with it. She pours a glass of water and walks over to the family room, where Marlena rests in her same spot on the sofa. "Sorry I smell like a skank. How are you today?"

"Pretty sore."

"Are you able to move around yet?"

"Not without embarrassing or killing myself. I'm working on it."

"So, home for a few more days, probably?"

"Yeah. Total suck. I'm bored as hell." Marlena turns gingerly. "So . . . I saw you outside. You're here early. What did Coach say?"

Kendall takes a long drink of water and then wipes at a drip from her lips. "We're done. It's over," she says. Shrugs. "He called around but couldn't get anybody to help us. Said we actually did pretty well, with a third of our high school on the team. I guess if you look at it that way, it does seem pretty crazy to think we'd find anybody else."

Marlena drops her head back onto her pillow. "Ugh. Crap. Jacián's going to murder me."

Kendall is quiet.

"Coach was trying to get a scout to show up to one of our games, trying to get him into one of the big soccer schools. He was deciding between UCLA and Stanford. Now I've messed up his chances at a scholarship." Her voice quivers. "Did he seem mad?"

Kendall remembers the scene in the truck and presses her lips together. "Not more than usual," she says lightly.

"Oh, God. I feel so bad." Marlena starts crying.

"Aw, shit," Kendall says, going over to her, sitting on the floor. "Come on, Marlena, it's not your fault. Nico's gone too. We've never lost two players at a time, and we were already down one from last year. It's not just you."

Jacián comes into the house and heads straight down a hallway, still wearing his cleats. Kendall hears a door shut and then the sound of water rushing through pipes on the other side of the wall as he turns on the shower. Her mind wanders for a minute and she shakes her head, embarrassed.

Marlena stares off out the window, a forlorn look on her face. Kendall laces and unlaces her fingers, holding each position to the count of six. When the phone rings, she stretches to reach it from the coffee table and hands it to Marlena.

"Hello?"

Marlena listens for a second and then says, "He just came in; he's in the shower. Have him call you back?" She pauses again and says, "Okay. Bye."

Kendall looks at Marlena, mildly curious.

"His girlfriend," she says. "Back in Arizona."

"Ah." Kendall picks up a magazine and pages through it idly. How Jacián managed to get a girlfriend is beyond her comprehension. "Is he always so ornery?"

"Nah. He just hates it here."

"So he tries to make everybody else's life miserable too?"

Marlena sighs. "I guess. But seriously, since we moved

here, nothing has gone right for him. Back in Arizona he had a weekend job at an indoor soccer arena, which he loved. He had a summer job at a soccer camp in the mountains that he had to give up because my parents made him work here on the ranch. He had his girlfriend, and a huge class AA school with a terrific soccer team.

"We finished school there and moved here, and within a week Sheriff Greenwood and the state police were knocking at the door and insinuating all sorts of crappy things. And then Grandpa put Jacián to work chasing down cattle and delivering meat. We didn't have a clue what we'd be doing here." She shifts, trying to get more comfortable. "He was pretty happy about the soccer team once he saw you all play, 'cause most of you are not bad, and it was so cool that Coach was doing so much to get a scout to come out to Bozeman for a game. But now that's over too." She sets the phone on the coffee table again. "And he's fighting with his girlfriend."

"He's fighting with everyone," Kendall says. The water shuts off.

Marlena shrugs. "He's really not a bad guy. He's actually got a very sweet side."

"Well, what about you?" Kendall asks. "What did you leave behind? Do you hate it here too?" Kendall feels a bit of protectiveness bubble up. She knows very well that Cryer's Cross is an odd kind of town and that things move a little slower out here than they do in big cities. She knows that riding your horse into town is unheard of in the rest of the country, but here it happens now and then with one of the old-timers.

Marlena smiles. "Me? Oh, I love it out here. It's so pretty with all the mountains, and the air is so clean, and you can see the stars. I'm glad we got to move here. Living in the hot, dirty city—it just wasn't my gig."

"Well, that's cool. Do you think your parents will stay out here? Like, for a year, or indefinitely?" Kendall hears a door open, and a moment later another door closes.

"I think we're here forever, as long as my grandfather is. It's kind of tradition with our culture, you know? It's very important to my mom that we take care of Grandpa now that he needs help."

"That's cool. I like that." Kendall hugs her knees and rests her chin on them. She likes Marlena. It's actually not bad having a girl to hang out with now and then.

Kendall's mother calls. "The car has a dead battery, and Dad's out in the back forty with the truck. He'll be out till late. Can you ask Hector to run you home?"

"Sure. He's not actually here right now."

"Well, maybe Marlena's parents or Jacián can do it, then? I'm kind of stuck here. If they can't, call me back and I'll walk over and we can walk home together. But the help are working extra hours for the next few weeks, and I'd like to offer them something to eat."

"It's cool, Mom. I'm sure I can get a ride. See you in a bit."

Kendall hangs up the phone. "So, uh," she says, "any chance your parents are coming home soon? My mom's car has a dead battery."

"Not until dark." Marlena turns her head and calls, "Jacián!"

"No, that's okay," Kendall says. "I can wait for Hector."

"Jacián!" she yells again, and then she says something in Spanish.

A moment later he comes down the hallway. "I'm going to tell Grandfather you said that," he says. "What do you want?"

"Kendall's mother's car has a dead battery so Kendall needs a ride home. And you also need to cook dinner for me, Mama said. I'm starving for a Whopper and fries or something. When are they going to get a fast-food place around here, huh?"

Kendall glances away. "Sorry, Jacián."

He's silent for a moment and she doesn't want to see the look on his face. "Okay," he says. "You ready to go?"

"Yeah." She is painfully conscious of her smelly sweat-damp clothes. She grabs her backpack and soccer bag and leans down for a quick hug. "Bye, Marlena. Hope you feel better tomorrow."

"Are you coming again?" Marlena asks, hopeful.

"I—I don't know. Maybe."

"I hope you can. Come tomorrow."

Jacián strides to the door and heads out to the barn. Kendall follows and gets in the truck as he starts it up.

"You reek," he says, wrinkling his nose.

"Thanks," Kendall says.

They travel in silence, Jacián taking much more care with the truck on this ride compared to the previous one.

Kendall thinks ahead to tomorrow's drive, and her anxiety kicks in. "Can you pick me up a few minutes earlier tomorrow?"

"Why?"

"I just . . . I just like to get to school a bit earlier."

"I like to get to school when it's time for school to start."

Kendall feels the stress building. Her mind starts whirring again, worrying about not getting the room set up the way it needs to be. Worrying about wanting to deal with seeing Nico's empty desk before the whole class gets there. She bites her lip and looks out the window. "Fine," she says. She's going to have to handle it.

He glances at her, brow furrowed, and then turns his eyes back to the road. A moment later he's pulling into the driveway. He drives up to the apron and stops next to Mrs. Fletcher's car. Puts the truck in park, rolls down the windows, turns off the ignition, and pops the hood.

Kendall looks at him. "What are you doing?"

"Can you get your mother's car keys, please?"

"She leaves them under the floor mat."

Jacián stops and stares at Kendall. Shakes his head a little. "I will never get used to this small-town crazy shit," he mutters. "It would have been stolen within ten minutes where we're from."

Kendall shrugs. "Not here."

"I suppose you don't lock your doors at night, either."

Kendall's eyes widen. "What do you mean by that? And yes, we do lock them. All of them. So don't bother testing it."

Jacián gives her a quizzical look. "I didn't mean anything by it." He gets out and pulls jumper cables from the big toolbox in the truck bed. "Sheesh, not you, too." His voice is bitter.

"No, I didn't mean—"

"Yes, you did." Roughly he pops the hood to the car and attaches the clips to the dead battery. Then he hands the other two to Kendall. "Don't let them touch," he says.

"I know that. I'm not stupid." Kendall clips the black and red pincers to the proper spots on the truck battery. "You want me to start up the truck?"

"Yeah." Jacián gets into Mrs. Fletcher's car.

Kendall starts it up, and when it's running strong, Jacián tries starting the car. It turns over on the second try.

He smiles to himself, satisfied. And then he gets out and retrieves the cables, disconnecting them in reverse order. "Okay, you're set. Let it run for a few." He winds up the cables and puts them back into the toolbox. "Take it for a drive, even."

"I can't. Remember?"

"Right," he says. "Forgot already. Must be a big pain in the ass."

Kendall gets out of the truck, leaving it running. "Yeah. Pretty much," she says and pauses. "Thanks for the ride, and for jumping my mom's car. She'll really appreciate that. I'll . . . see you in the morning, then."

He slides into the seat and closes the door. Leans his elbow out the window. "Bring your soccer gear if you want. If you're coming over after." He puts the truck in gear.

Kendall feels her face get warm. "Maybe," she says lightly. "And hey," she remembers out loud, "your girlfriend called while you were in the shower. Marlena forgot to tell you."

Jacián's face doesn't change. "Oh. All right," he says. "Thanks." He pulls his arm inside and backs up, turning around. Drives off without another word.

WE

Achingly close. We sense the warmth but We can't reach it. Want. Need! Thirty-five, one hundred. Thirty-five, one hundred. We cry out to be touched, fear gripping Our scratchy voices. Fifty cold years in the darkness, boiling in regret. Come closer! We want you, more than We wanted the last. Torturously.

Please.
Save me.

FOURTEEN

He's early.

Kendall's ready, sitting by the picture window, think-ing about Nico, and her heart almost breaks, wishing he were here. Wishing she could talk to him. When she sees the cloud of dust at the end of the driveway, she thinks it's him, before reality bashes her in the head yet again.

By the time Jacián's truck reaches the house, she's already kissed her mother good-bye and is waiting. She hops into the truck. Wants to thank him for coming early, but feels suddenly embarrassed about bringing it up again. She wonders, briefly, why she allows herself to get flustered by him. He's just so . . . unreadable.

At school she passes old Mr. Greenwood on his way

out, and she rushes to take care of as many things as possible before Jacián catches up to her. She gets the wastebasket, markers, window locks, and drapes aligned before she hears his footsteps. Then she straightens the desks one by one. Feeling relief as she passes her fingers over each one, reading the graffiti like it's comfort food for her brain. Not even caring that he's staring at her.

When she gets to the senior section, Jacián is already sitting at his desk, reading. His desk is slightly crooked. Not enough for the average person to notice, but for Kendall it's like a musical note that is slightly off pitch, playing constantly. She itches to ask him to move but knows how weird that would be. She knows people without OCD have a really hard time understanding it. And she's okay with that. Still. She'll wait until he gets up. She finishes the desks around her—Eli's, Travis's, Brandon's, and she can't bear to look at Nico's quite yet. She glances at Jacián's desk, and she's bothered beyond ordinary by it today. But people are starting to stream into the room.

Without a word, and still reading his book, he stands and steps out of the way. "Go on, then," he says.

She gives him a look of surprise, but he doesn't notice. Hesitates and pinches her lips together, debating. Then she swiftly adjusts his desk so it's perfectly aligned. Slides into her own desk chair and takes a deep breath, letting it out slowly. Almost done. "Thank you," she says.

His mouth twitches, but he keeps reading.

She turns to Nico's desk, more prepared today for him to not be there. It still feels awful. She moves the desk slightly, lovingly, to line it up with hers. Runs her fingers across it, tentatively. Lifts the lid and looks inside, but there's nothing in there anymore, so she closes it again. It's so cold and stark. Empty. She reads the graffiti, but it all means something different this time with him gone. It's Nico's desk, but there's something unusual, something niggling at the back of her mind that she can't quite figure out.

And then she realizes what it is. A new phrase etched into the top of the desk, but it doesn't look new. It looks ten or twenty or fifty years old, like all the other graffiti. Kendall leans to the right to get a closer look. Definitely not a fresh one. If Nico had done it, it wouldn't look so smooth.

Ms. Hinkler begins class by passing out papers. Kendall glances around to make sure she's not acting too weird, and then she leans over again. It's near the center of his desk, and it says, without a doubt:

Please.
Save me.

How strange that she hasn't noticed it before. How could she have missed it?

All day, she doesn't hear a thing that Ms. Hinkler is saying. She can't concentrate, wondering about the desk, the graffiti. She studies it, focuses all her attention on it. Remembers that this desk isn't one of the desks that has been in this classroom forever. It is just as old as all the others, but it had been kept in storage until it was needed. Old Mr. Greenwood brought it upstairs last spring when another one broke.

She knows who used to have this desk. Tiffany Quinn.

And then, after the schoolroom had a cleaning over the summer, the desk ended up as Nico's.

Kendall draws in a sharp breath, loud enough to make Jacián look over. He raises his eyebrows in a silent question.

Kendall looks at him for a moment, and then smiles shakily and waves him off. "Nothing," she says.

And really, when she thinks about it rationally, it truly is nothing. Nothing more than a strange coincidence.

At lunch she stays inside and studies the desk, wanting to be sure, but she's not entirely certain what she wants to be sure of. Finally she takes out a piece of notebook paper. Writes down the things she's sure of, and what she's almost sure of. In the "sure of" column:

- Tiffany Quinn and Nico Cruz each were using this desk when they disappeared

- The desk in question has new graffiti on it that looks old

She erases the second point and puts it in the "almost sure" category.

Then she erases the first point, accidentally ripping the paper with her eraser in her haste, and puts that in the "almost sure" category too. Because now she's not entirely sure about anything.

All afternoon her brain buzzes with thoughts she can't control. She wants to yell, wants to make them stop. But they whip around in an endless loop. After a while she just puts her head down on her desk and gives up.

"Kendall."

"Yeah?"

"Time to go."

Kendall sits up slowly, wearily. She has no idea what Ms. Hinkler has talked about all day. Doesn't care, either. Her body feels like it's filled with lead. She sits for a minute, realizing everybody is already gone except for Jacián. She slips out of her seat and grabs her backpack and bag.

"Are you okay?"

Kendall nods. "I think a lot of junk just caught up with

me." She glances over her shoulder at Nico's desk as they walk to the door. "I'm starting to imagine things."

Jacián pushes open the door and holds it for Kendall to walk through. He doesn't say anything.

"How did you know?" she asks.

"Know what?"

"Know to stand up this morning so I could straighten your desk."

"Oh, that." Jacián gets into the truck. "It was pretty obvious just by watching you."

"Oh."

"And Marlena told me."

"Told you what?" Kendall's starting to feel paranoid.

"That you told her you have OCD."

"Oh." Kendall can't think of anything else to say. She's a little bit mad that Marlena squawked about it, but thinking back, Kendall hadn't said not to.

Jacián gets into the truck. "Have you always had a problem with it?"

Kendall eyes him suspiciously. "Why?"

He starts it up as Kendall gets in on the passenger side. "Just making conversation. Sheesh. You really are a little paranoid, aren't you? Is that part of the OCD, or is it just natural?"

"There you go, being jerkish again. Is that just natural for you?" She turns her face toward her window so he doesn't see her grin. She's glad he's being normal about it.

He sighs and pulls out of the school parking area. "You're coming home with me, right?"

"Yeah."

"Look. I know about OCD. I was a junior counselor at a soccer camp for two summers before we came here. I had a lot of campers with secrets. You're not the only one in the world with it, you know."

Kendall humphs. "Feels like it sometimes."

"Aw, poor you."

"Shut up."

He shrugs.

They get to Hector's, pull into the barn, and get out of the truck. Jacián picks up the soccer balls. "You bring your clothes?"

Kendall debates. She has them, but she doesn't like where the previous conversation went. Still, she feels like a slug, and her brain desperately needs a break. "Yeah."

They walk up the porch steps and go inside. "There's a bathroom upstairs you can use," he says. "Or just use Marlena's room. She's not using it until she can actually get up there."

Kendall sees Marlena with her eyes closed, lying on the sofa. Walks softly upstairs and changes, then tiptoes back outside so she doesn't wake her friend. Jacián follows a minute later. They stretch in silence. Kendall feels the pull in her back, her thighs, and scolds herself for not dancing at all lately. *But when your best friend since birth disappears, I guess maybe sometimes you forget to dance.* She eases down into the splits and leans over her right knee.

"Does the workout help?"

Kendall is distracted from her thoughts. "Help what?"

"Your OCD."

"Yes."

"That's what I thought. The kids I worked with—they were always so much . . . I don't know. Happier? Calmer, maybe, after playing hard all day."

Kendall is taken aback by his attempt at conversation. She's skeptical, unable to figure out why he's suddenly willing to talk, but she's too tired to question it. "It definitely helps me. During, mostly, but a little bit after, too." Kendall shifts and bows over her other knee. "Wish I could play all year."

"Why can't you?"

Kendall looks at him. "Uh . . . because of the snow?"

"Oh. Forgot about that."

"Yeah."

"So what do you do when it snows?"

She gets an unexpected lump in her throat, thinking about ice fishing with Nico, snowshoeing with Nico, skiing in the mountains with Nico. And dancing. Not with

Nico. "Dance," she says. "Theatre. Only once so far, but I want to do it again someday." She gets to her feet and grabs a soccer ball, kicking it wide and chasing after it, ending the conversation before it gets dangerous. She's tired of crying.

They work on their own for a while. It's a lot more comfortable today than it was yesterday, and eventually they fall into a scrimmage. Jacián's bigger, stronger, and can run a little faster, but Kendall is a tiny bit quicker changing direction on a dime. If she can get past him, she's got it made.

Problem is getting past him.

Jacián plays rough, just this side of dirty. He always has, and he doesn't go easy on girls—not on Marlena or on Kendall. It's something Kendall noticed the first day, and she actually really appreciates that. She always tries to take him down too. Can't let him get too cocky. And while she plays, he is the enemy. Kendall focuses all her brainpower on the win.

She doesn't even notice when Marlena hobbles out the door with Hector and they sit on the porch, watching as Kendall goes in for the kill shot. She races Jacián to the ball, every muscle in her body screaming, stretched to its limit. He steps in, and she slams into him. Her body flies and she lands on her back, hard. It knocks the wind out of her and she lies there, stunned for a moment, before she starts fighting for air. It's the worst feeling in the world, trying to breathe but not being able to. At least Jacián went down too.

She rolls onto her side, and they lie on the grass, heaving.

When Kendall can speak, she says, "You suck."

Jacián grins at the sky.

Later, Kendall joins Hector and Marlena on the porch. She sits on the steps and guzzles a giant glass of water, listening to Hector and Marlena talk.

"Aren't you going into town today to visit with old Mr. Greenwood?" Marlena asks.

"Not today. I have some paperwork to take care of."

"What will he think if you don't show up?"

"Ah, he'll be fine. It's not the first time. Sometimes he doesn't show up either. We are good friends for a long time and understand each other."

Kendall turns. "I think it's cute that you sit together and never talk to each other, like an old married couple."

"Ha! We talk sometimes. I didn't know the whole town was worried about us." He grins.

"I don't think I've ever heard old Mr. Greenwood say more than a few words at school, like if he's yelling at us to clean up or whatever," Kendall says. "He's kind of cranky.

How long have you known him? Has he always been that way?"

Hector shakes his head. "It's been a long time. Since we were about like you two . . . maybe a few years younger, each." He gets a strange look in his eyes.

Marlena leans in. "Did you meet here? Did you always live here, Grandpa?"

"We met here in Montana, yes." He turns to explain to Kendall, "I was born in Texas, and my parents only spoke Spanish, so I didn't learn English until I went to school. They were good field-workers, and we migrated here one spring to work when I was fourteen. I was . . ." He pauses. "I was not a good boy. I had a lot of troubles with other kids."

"Because . . . ?" Marlena demands.

"Because . . . Well, partly because I am Mexican. Here in Montana there were Native Americans and Caucasians. Not so many Mexicans."

"So what happened?" Kendall turns around on the steps so she can watch his face.

"I got into fights. And my parents couldn't have me doing that. They worked very hard for long hours, and I was bad. So they found me a new place to live."

Marlena's mouth drops open. "You mean, like, with another family? With the Greenwoods? Is that how you became friends?"

"No, no . . . nothing like that." Hector glances at his watch. "My goodness, I have to go. I have to get some invoices together pronto for Jacián. He has deliveries tonight. Miss Kendall, do you need a ride home?" He slowly eases out of his chair.

"My mother's going to pick me up at six, if that's okay."

"Aren't you all busy harvesting those delicious potatoes? Seems like the right time."

"Yeah," Kendall says guiltily. "They let me off the hook because of Nico. They think it's good I'm spending time talking with friends. Whatever that means."

"It means you're not all alone and brooding on a tractor or in a field," Hector says.

"Whatever it means, it's practically the first September I've had off from harvesting since I could walk," Kendall says. "Still . . . I'd rather have Nico back."

"It's very hard to lose a friend at your age. I have been through it," Hector says. He shakes his head and shuffles into the house. "Be careful out there, Miss Kendall. I'd be sick if we lost you, too, or anyone."

When Kendall's mother picks her up, she hands Kendall a letter. "It's from Juilliard," Mrs. Fletcher says.

Kendall stares at it, her stomach jumping into her throat. Takes it, not quite sure how she's supposed to feel.

Slips her finger under the flap and slides it across. Pulls out the folded piece of paper and opens it.

She reads for a moment with held breath, and then skims the rest of the letter. Lets it drop into her lap.

"It's a no." Kendall gazes out the car window, focusing on the distant mountains. Mrs. Fletcher squeezes Kendall's hand and starts driving home.

It's what they thought. What she'd expected. And to be honest, Kendall hasn't thought about it much since Nico disappeared. It doesn't really seem to matter anymore. Nothing does.

Still, she wonders, why does it hurt so much?

That night Kendall checks all the doors and windows six times each before she goes to bed. She's exhausted, but her mind is revving up again, recalling everything that happened today. Blocking out the Juilliard letter as best she can. But it doesn't matter, because her brain keeps bringing her back to earlier in the day.

All she can think about is one thing.

Desks.

WE

Only a faltering brush of warmth today.

Cold, so cold. We move Our cast-iron anchors, creaking, slowly inching across the floor, hours and hours of strain in search of heat and life. Now butting against a soulless We, now pushing the dead one out of Our way into the empty space. We breathe, ache, rest, strain again. We make Our move. Stalking the next soul to trade for one of Us.

FIFTEEN

When Kendall and Jacián get to school, she senses it, and a shiver goes down her spine—something's off. She moves through her rituals and straightens the desks. When she gets to the senior section, she stops.

"These desks are switched," she says. "Nico's and Travis's. Did you switch them?"

Jacián frowns. "You've been with me the whole time. Did you see me switch them?"

Kendall wrestles Travis's desk out of the way and moves Nico's desk back to where it belongs. "Who could have done this?" She rips her fingers through her hair, distressed. "This is Nico's desk. It's staying right here next to me. Totally not funny."

"It was probably the janitor moving desks to clean. So. it got moved. No big deal." Jacián goes back to his book. "I'd ask how you even noticed it's not Nico's desk, but I'm scared to know the answer."

"I know all the desks," Kendall says, straightening Travis's. "I have them—"

"No." Jacián holds up his hand. "What did I just say?"

Kendall stops abruptly as the rest of the class trickles in. She takes a closer look at the spot on Nico's desk that had the new/old graffiti yesterday. It's still there, same as before. Looking like it's been there for years. She shakes her head. Must have just missed that one, or forgotten it somehow. It's not like she's been exactly stable the past few weeks. And maybe because it says *help*, she actually really noticed it in a different way this time. Almost as if Nico were crying out for it.

But, like a good portion of Kendall's thoughts, that one is just ridiculous.

Halfway through the day, when she's supposed to be writing a book report, she stops short and lays her pen down. It really hits her. She's not going to Juilliard.

She has no reason to ever dance again. Add to that, no reason to play soccer again. No reason to do anything without those things in her life. Without Nico. She slumps to her desk, suddenly very, very tired. On her notebook she doodles the word "LOST," making the last letter dangle precipitously down the right margin.

Jacián glances at her notebook. Frowns. But says nothing.

Day after day after day goes by in black and white for Kendall now. She puts herself in a mind-numbing routine of school, farm, homework, sleep. She rides silently in the pickup to and from school with Jacián and Marlena, making small talk but not remembering any of it. Sitting quietly at her desk, moving automatically through the days, just getting by, and doing whatever her OCD tells her to do, no more, no less.

There is no more visiting Hector's ranch once Marlena comes back to school. Marlena starts hanging out with the other tenth graders, who begin to get to know her, help her out when she needs it.

There's no more soccer with Jacián either. Kendall's parents need her desperately on the farm. It's the height of harvest, and Kendall has work to do. Everything is one dull event after another now. She plunges her hands into freezing water, pulling leaves and bad potatoes off a belt for hours every day after school, and all she can do is think.

The thing is, for Kendall it just doesn't matter. Nico is gone. Juilliard is no longer a goal. There's no future with either one of her two favorite things—both dreams shattered within a matter of days. What else is there to think about? The truth is that Kendall might be tough on the outside. She can take a hit, and she can stand up for herself. But inside, in her scared heart and in her stupid, unstoppable brain, Kendall knows that she will stay in Cryer's Cross forever. She will work on this farm until she inherits it someday. She will probably marry somebody like Eli Greenwood or Travis Shank and have children who play soccer on a too-small team until they graduate.

Or maybe not. Maybe she'll shake up the town and stay single, adopt a baby or two, and just hide out at the farm.

And wait.

Wait for Nico to come back.

WE

Sapped. Our energy drained, only to be manhandled away. The rage! Oh, but the touch . . . It's there. It's near, within reach. We must become stronger. Draw Our next victim to Us from afar.

We simmer, day after day, hoarding what strength remains. And We wait.

SIXTEEN

By mid-October, Kendall is stuck in a loop of depressing thoughts that won't leave her. Lost without a goal, lost without her best friend, lost in a thousand acres of potatoes. There is no meaning, no plan. No sense in anything. All she can do is just plod through it. Get the work done so she can get up again the next day and start over. Go to bed before eleven so the missing phone call doesn't hurt so much. Get to school early so she can do what she has to do, her OCD ball and chain dictating her every waking hour.

Every night she stands by the upstairs window and looks out toward the Cruz farm. She doesn't know why.

It's just . . . for memory's sake. And every night it is a dark and lonely view. "I'll say I'm your girlfriend if you just come back," she says, her breath fogging up the window. "I promise."

Tonight she sees a vehicle go down the gravel road slowly, and she watches its brake lights flicker as it navigates potholes. When it's gone from view, the world is dark again except for the stars and the harvest moon that casts an orange glow over the fields. "I know you can see this moon too, Nico," she whispers. "Somewhere."

Just as she turns away from the window, something moving halfway down the driveway catches her eye. She squints and makes out a figure standing there. Her heart jumps. Could it be Nico? She stares harder. It can't be! In a daze she moves down the stairs, telling herself it's not him. Someone would have called with the news. By the time she reaches the door, she's growing scared. If it's not Nico, then who is standing in their driveway at this hour?

Kendall stops short of flying through the door to gather her senses. Maybe it's the abductor, ready to grab her. She sucks in a breath and slowly pushes aside the curtain of the window next to the front door and she peers out, trying to get her eyes to adjust to the darkness again.

But there's no one there. No one that she can see, anyway. Not with so many places to hide . . . long grass, trees, barns, tractors to hide behind. She spins around and runs back upstairs to the window. And from there she sees a figure—a man, she's sure—running away, cutting the corner of the front field.

She flies over to her phone and dials Eli Greenwood's number. Sheriff Greenwood answers. "Hello."

"I just saw a man watching my house." She's breathless.

"Mrs. Fletcher?"

"No, it's Kendall. There was a man standing halfway down our driveway just a couple minutes ago, and I thought it might be Nico, but then he turned and ran away when I went downstairs for a closer look."

Sheriff Greenwood is quiet. "I'll head out. Can you give me any description? Do you think it really was Nico?"

Kendall hesitates. "I did at first, but that was probably because I was thinking about him. If it was Nico, I'm sure he would have come to the door. So it couldn't be." *Could it?* She's so confused.

"I'll take a look. Could be somebody out for a walk. Just lock up tight, all right? Your parents home?"

"Yes. They're sleeping."

"You try to get some sleep too now. Hear?"

"Yes, sir."

They hang up.

Kendall rechecks all the door locks and windows and goes back upstairs to her room. She lies in bed but knows there's no sleeping now. She thinks about waking her parents, but in the middle of harvest they are exhausted. Besides, what could they do? The guy ran away.

Her heart is in her throat and she can't stop getting up to check her bedroom window over and over. Because the way it works in her brain, if somebody breaks in, it'll be her fault for not checking the lock enough times.

When she finally falls into a troubled sleep, she dreams about Nico.

Kidnapping and stabbing her to death.

SEVENTEEN

In the morning the ride to school is awkward and silent. After Kendall does her school rituals, Jacián pulls her aside.

"Can I talk to you for a minute?" He looks troubled.

"Sure," Kendall says, without enthusiasm. She's tired from lack of sleep and paranoid about the kidnapper on the loose.

They step outside and around to the back of the school as students begin arriving.

"What's so important that you can't say it in the class-room?"

Jacián presses his lips together, and then he says,

"Look. I don't know how to say this without you freaking out at me. Can I just ask you to listen until I'm through?"

Kendall shifts and narrows her eyes. "What? Why would I freak out?"

"Last night . . . that was me in your driveway. Sheriff Greenwood told me I could explain it myself, and he's going to call you this evening."

"What? What were you doing watching me? God!"

"Please . . ."

Kendall is quiet, but her brain is on fire with new fearful thoughts.

"I was out for a walk. I couldn't sleep, and I had a really shitty evening, and the sky was awesome and, well, yeah. I went past your house and saw the upstairs all lit up from the road. On my way back it was darker, but I could see your silhouette in the window, just standing there. And, I don't know . . . I just started walking down your driveway for some insane reason. I was feeling bad, and I figured you were too, and so I thought maybe you'd want to . . . I don't know. Talk or something. It was stupid." His eyes are hard and he looks off toward the parking lot.

Kendall stares at him.

"Then I saw you disappear and I sort of came to my senses, realized how late it was, and how you can't stand me anyway so why the hell would you want to talk, and I got scared and took off running. I swear that's the truth."

His jaw is set. "Greenwood picked me up five minutes later and questioned me for more than an hour. Then he told me he believed me and drove me home. He said he wanted me to tell you it was me. And that he's going to call you after school to make sure I told you. And that . . ." He pauses. "And that you can press charges for trespassing if you want."

Kendall doesn't know what to say.

Jacián shoves one hand in his pocket and rakes through his hair with the other, leaving it standing up wildly. "I just figured you were hurting. I mean, after the way you've been acting the last few weeks. And thought . . . well. Fuck it. Never mind. It was a stupid thing to do." He sighs. "I'm sorry, Kendall. Okay? I didn't mean to scare you. Hell."

Kendall looks at the dirt. Shocked. Embarrassed, a little, but angry, too. And there's something sad about it all . . . sad that it wasn't Nico out there, even after her nightmare. But still, she doesn't explode like she thought she would when he first started talking. She just turns away. "Okay." She shrugs and walks back into school, leaving him standing there.

A minute later he slides into the desk next to her and stares straight ahead.

They don't talk all day.

Kendall just stares at Nico's desk, thinking. Thinking about how Tiffany Quinn sat there and disappeared. And how Nico sat there and disappeared. And now it's all she can think about. What would happen if she sat there? Maybe disappearing would be better than all this. And at the very least, sitting there would be like wearing one of Nico's shirts. A comfort, being where he was. Maybe it could help her get over him.

Maybe tomorrow she'll sit there.

Things are tense in the truck on the way home. Unaware, Marlena chatters about how she can't wait until she gets her cast off, and Jacián and Kendall stare straight ahead until they're all sitting in front of Kendall's house.

"Thanks," Kendall mumbles as usual. As she slams the truck door shut, she catches Jacián's eye and sees the fear in it. He swallows hard, his Adam's apple bobbing, and then he glances away as Marlena says goodbye through the window in the midst of her babbling. Kendall stands there for a minute, puzzled, and then turns toward the house. It's not until she's outside harvesting potatoes that it dawns on her why he had such a scared look in his eyes.

He's from a big city. A place where people steal cars if you don't make it too difficult for them not to. He really thinks she and her family are going to press charges against him for trespassing.

Kendall stops what she's doing for a moment, and she

nearly laughs out loud for the first time in weeks. Poor Jacián. He's probably been worried sick about it all day.

She thinks about what he said. How he thought maybe she was hurting, and tears start leaking from her eyes. She didn't know the guy actually had a heart underneath all that anger. But the only person she can talk to who would fix her pain is Nico.

On their way back to the house from the fields, Kendall tells her mother what happened the night before.

"You should have woken me up," Mrs. Fletcher says with a frown.

"It wasn't that big of a deal," Kendall says, and today, during daylight, and knowing the truth, it really doesn't feel like a big deal. "And you guys are working so hard, I didn't want to wake you up. So, do you want to press charges against Jacián?"

"Don't be ridiculous. What would people think of us? What a terrible thing to do to that poor boy. After all he's done for you, driving you around."

Kendall shrugs. But it's comforting to know her mother thinks he's not a bad guy.

When Sheriff Greenwood calls, he tells the same story as Jacián told, in lesser detail. "Your parents want to press charges for trespassing? If so, I need to talk to them," he says. "I can't see you all doing it, but it's your right."

"No, I talked with my mother. We don't want to do that."

"Good. I'll let him know. He'll be happy to hear it. I'll tell him to stay out of people's driveways at night."

"Okay. Thanks."

They hang up.

Mrs. Fletcher smiles at Kendall from the kitchen, where she warms up leftover beef stew in the microwave. "So, Kendall."

Kendall sighs. "Yes?"

"Have you been thinking about other colleges?"

She flops her head in her hands. "I'm too tired and starving to have this conversation. Can we talk about it some other time?"

Mrs. Fletcher stirs the stew. "I'm a little worried about you."

"I'm fine. I'm just . . . trying to work through it."

Mrs. Fletcher gives Kendall a long look. "Okay. Life will be back to normal in a couple weeks, when harvest is done. Then we'll talk about the future."

Kendall doesn't respond. Back to normal? Without Nico, life will never be normal again.

WE

With time, We grow strong. We savor the strength. Taste the nearness of life.

The time will come. Soon. We strain to reach Our invisible grasp beyond the grainy surface, holding in fifty years' worth of screams.

EIGHTEEN

She stares at Nico's desk all morning, butterflies in her stomach. Afraid to sit there. Compelled to try. She tries to laugh off her fear. It was just a ridiculous coincidence. If she says it out loud, it's laughable. Nobody would believe that a desk has anything to do with the disappearances. It's absurd.

Still, the thought whirrs through her brain. She should sit there to prove it isn't the desk.

Next to her, Jacián is pointedly not looking at her, though this morning on the way in to school he managed a gruff "Thank you" for not pressing charges. But Kendall takes no notice of him. She rests her head on her desk as usual, knowing Ms. Hinkler won't call on her. The teacher hasn't asked Kendall a direct question since Nico disappeared.

When everyone leaves to eat lunch outside on this cool fall day, Kendall stays inside. Slowly she stands, heart pounding. She steps over to Nico's desk and then she slides into it. She closes her eyes and holds her breath. And then she moves her arms around the desktop to embrace it. *Nico*, she thinks, *are you here?*

She rests her head on the desk and lets out her breath, then tries to relax and think about him. Think about all their good times. Lets the memories flood her brain.

It's harmless. She is still in the room, sitting in Nico's desk. Still here, not disappeared. After a while Kendall sits up and runs her fingers over the desktop. She reads each line of graffiti as she often does, but it feels different from this angle. She gets lost in the words as they swirl around in her mind, and she tries to make them sound right, like a poem would sound. A jumble of words, written over the course of fifty years by dozens of authors.

She lands on the plea. Probably some bored student watching the clock tick away slowly, waiting for something awesome that won't come until the end of the day.

Please.
Save me.

She traces the letters and wonders again why she hadn't seen them before.

And then she hears a whisper. *Please. Save me.* Like wind in leaves, so faint that Kendall is sure she made a mistake.

Her body tingles, and she feels the back of her neck prickle. She jerks her hand away and looks around the room. "Who's there?"

Her heart pumps at top speed. Tentatively she reaches toward the words again and slides her forefinger across them. Her whole body floods with adrenaline, like being high on some crazy drug, and she closes her eyes. In her ear the delicious whisper comes again, more urgent this time. *Please, save me!*

Kendall is drawn in. The euphoric feeling is almost overwhelming, like running too far too fast, but she craves more. She leans over the words, her finger tracing the letters, and in her ears the whisper, over and over.

When she pulls her fingers away, the buzz of the high slowly ebbs. She sits for a moment as the whispers grow too soft to hear, and then she opens her eyes and realizes why the whispers were so beautiful.

The voice was Nico's.

Immediately Kendall's OCD kicks in. Fear grips her and she can't seem to get out of the desk fast enough. She nearly tips it over in her haste to get away, knocking the books from her own desk just as the lunching students return.

"What the heck was that?" she mutters under her breath, scrambling to pick up her books. Her brain is screaming at her to get away. Get away from the wonderful evil.

She knows that whatever it was, it wasn't real. It can't be real. It must be some weird grief thing, where you hear the voice of someone who has passed and really think it's him. But it was just so strong. She catches her breath as Jacián comes in and sits down. Kendall slides back into her desk, heart still racing, trying to make sense of what just happened. Knowing it was all just emotion, grief. Feelings taking over, teasing her. Reminding her of how good it felt to be with Nico.

"It was never *that* good," she mutters. Her temples pound.

"What?" Jacián says.

Kendall startles and turns to look at him. His brown eyes are flecked with yellow, and his eyebrows knit together, concerned. "Nothing," she says. "Just . . . mumbling."

Jacián keeps looking at her. "Just mumbling," he says.

"That's what I said."

He shrugs and pulls his notebook out of his backpack. "Look," he says, "whenever you're done with those potatoes, I could really use a soccer partner. If you're not still mad. I mean, you can just come home with us whenever."

Kendall's brain is still buzzing. She edges away from Nico's desk, toward Jacián. "I'm too tired to even think of playing."

"That's because you're not playing."

"What do I have to play for?"

Jacián stares at her for a long moment. Then he just shakes his head lightly and turns to face the front of the classroom.

They sit there in silence and wait for Ms. Hinkler to start the afternoon work. For the next three hours Kendall can't stop thinking about what happened with the desk.

And about hearing Nico's voice.

By evening Kendall has reasoned away what happened. Her grief is playing tricks with her brain. Sure, her connection with Nico was strong—they were like twins in a way, the way they grew up and were always together. Of course she's going to think she hears his voice now and then. It's spooky, but it's completely natural. And totally explainable. And completely sad.

It just makes her feel so lonely.

She lies in bed, window checked six times, moonlight streaming in through the soft white curtains. So lonely her arms ache with no one to hold.

WE

Too much!

We pull back, suck in Our hypnotic venom, but it's too late. The heat, the life is gone. Too strong, too desperate. And you . . . unwilling? Nonmalleable? We curse now in the dark, quiet room. Our only option is to move.

We groan and creak, inching along, Our built-up strength leaking out with each motion.

There is no other choice for Us.

NINETEEN

He's alone in the morning in the pouring rain.

"Where's Marlena?" Kendall asks, climbing into the truck.

Jacián chews on a toothpick, his dark eyes squinting through the sheets of water as his wipers fly from side to side. He flips the gearshift into drive. "Bozeman, getting a checkup at the doctor's today. They're taking the cast off."

"Oh, that's right. Cool."

"She'll still have to wear one of those boot things for a couple weeks."

"Ew. Hideous. Serious fashion emergency."

Jacián laughs and glances at her. "My parents and grandfather would like you and your family to come for dinner Sunday to celebrate. It's Marlena's sixteenth birthday. Can your family get away?"

"Just us?"

"No. Greenwoods too, and Marlena's new sophomore friends. And maybe some others. I don't know. My grandfather is going to call your parents but I thought I'd mention it." He slows at the four-way stop in town and peers through the weather. "Maybe we can scrimmage with Eli and a few of the others if they come." He looks at her again, and his eyes are so earnest.

Kendall half smiles. "I brought my clothes today," she says. She pats her backpack. "Mom told me I'm too mopey and she's giving me the day off. I packed them up before I looked outside and saw this mess."

"You did?" He sounds shocked. Pleased. "A little rain is nothing," he says, a smile playing on his lips. He pulls into the parking lot. "Let me know about Sunday. Two o'clock. Or, you know—tell Marlena, or whatever."

"I will."

He turns the truck off, and their collective breath steams up the windows. They sit for a minute, timing the rain, but it's not letting up. Kendall looks over at Jacián. "Ready?"

He nods, and they make a mad dash for the school, splashing through the muddy parking lot to the doorway.

"Ever hear of concrete around here?" Jacián asks,

looking at his jeans in disgust. They stomp their feet and go inside the school. "Or tar. Tar works too. They make roads out of it, and parking lots. . . ."

"Shut it."

He goes into the classroom first and stops short. "Do you, like, need to be the first to enter the room too?"

"No." She eyes him suspiciously to see if he's mocking her, but he appears serious.

"Just wondering. I knew a kid at camp who always needed to be in the front. He'd go around getting all upset and saying 'I'm the front! I'm the front!' and everybody was mean to him, thinking he was just trying to be first in line all the time. They didn't understand."

"It's different for everybody." Kendall shakes the rain out of her hair and starts on her rituals.

A moment later Jacián says, "Hey, Kendall?"

"Yeah?"

"I'm not positive, but I think Nico's desk is switched again."

Kendall's stomach twists. "Seriously?" She finishes up the curtains and walks over to Jacián. "You're right."

She looks around to see which one it's switched with. "What the hell," she whispers. "This is so not normal." She looks at Jacián. "I know you probably think this is dumb that I'm all hung up over this, but this never happens. The desks only get moved out of the room for major cleaning during the summer, so they're all scrambled in the fall. But they never get moved out of sequence the rest of the year. Never." Kendall drops her backpack and wildly searches the room for Nico's desk. She finds it in the sophomore section and wrenches it back as Jacián moves the other one out of the way.

Jacián touches her arm. "I don't think it's dumb for you to want Nico's desk to be there, next to you. Waiting for when he comes back," he says.

Kendall stops. Swallows hard. Trying to decide if she still believes he'll come back.

Jacián drops his hand from her arm and steps out of the way so she can pull the desk back into its proper place. He lifts up the other one and moves it fluidly to the empty spot.

She's still looking at him. He doesn't meet her gaze. "Thank you," she says. Stupid hot tears spring to her eyes. "That's probably the nicest thing anybody's said to me in all these weeks."

"Well, that sucks."

Kendall pulls it together and then narrows her eyes. "Why are you being nice to me?" She slides into her seat and sits sideways to face him. "Hmm?"

He looks into her eyes for a long moment, and she sees something there. Loneliness, or compassion . . . something incredibly human that she hadn't noticed before. "I just want to play some soccer," he says lightly. "Figure it's time to bribe you with my charismatic personality."

"Oh," she says. Her voice is hollow, and she puzzles over how disappointed she feels that he told the truth. She should have known he wanted something.

Students arrive in exploding bursts because of the rain. Kendall turns away, rests her head on her desk, looking at Nico's. She doesn't see Jacián slump in his seat. Doesn't see him close his eyes and shake his head, doesn't hear the curse under his breath.

It rains off and on throughout the day. Kendall is tempted to sit at Nico's desk, but she doesn't want to do it when anybody is around. When it rains, everybody stays inside all day, eating lunch at their desks, so there's no chance.

After school the rain has stopped, and Jacián and Kendall step gingerly to the truck, taking care not to soak the interior with mud, but it's pointless. The air is crisp.

Jacián starts the engine and throws an arm across the backseat, looking over his shoulder preparing to back up. His fingers brush the tips of Kendall's hair. She moves closer to her door. "Where to?" he asks.

She looks at him. "You too chickenshit to play in this?"

"No."

"Well, then. Let's go play."

The car doesn't move. His mouth twitches. "I didn't

mean what I said, you know. About being nice just so you'll play. It was just a joke."

Kendall bites her lip. She can feel his eyes on her, and she's not altogether sure what the churning feeling is inside her gut. Maybe it's just that some of her numbness is finally wearing off.

When it's clear Kendall has no response, Jacián backs out of the parking area and picks his way slowly down the muddy road toward Hector's, looking for new potholes to avoid.

They change inside the empty house and meet on the soaked, spongy grass. Kendall is glad she brought a thick sweatshirt, though one good fall and it'll soak through. A little thrill goes through her at the thought of the fresh air and exercise, and it's always fun to play in the rain, no matter what Coach says.

It's been too long since she's played, she knows that. She starts stretching.

They warm up, jogging in place. Kendall's hair flops all around, and she's mad she forgot a ponytail holder to keep her hair out of her face. They do a few exercises, dribbling, setting each other up. Each of them taking it slow, cautious of the sodden turf. Nobody needs a groin pull, that's for sure.

As Kendall gets used to the conditions, she takes more chances. Her intensity multiplies, and soon she is in the zone—the brain-quieting zone where all of the whir-ring thoughts slow and stop for a while. It's such a relief. Flooded with mind-dizzying endorphins, Kendall takes the ball, and Jacián, to task. She doesn't even notice when it starts sprinkling and then full-out raining again. All she knows is that she feels relief for the first time in weeks.

Her depression dissipates and her mind goes some-where else, somewhere quiet and peaceful, where nothing is there to trouble her. It's like she's floating as she darts around Jacián and takes the ball to the goal, leaving him breathless and staring at her.

Again and again she gets the better of him on this slick surface. It's like the more difficult things are, the more Kendall can concentrate and focus. Her brain knows only one thing now. To take the ball around the opposition, past the enemy, and put it in the net. So simple, yet so complex.

When the enemy gets the better of her, messes with her mojo, she doesn't think. She charges.

At top speed Kendall chases after Jacián. She pulls alongside him and grabs him around the waist, tackling him as the ball goes off, out of bounds. He slips and falls to a knee with a grunt and splashes in the soaking, muddy yard, grabbing Kendall's arm as he goes down. He's not going down alone.

Kendall lands on top of him.

"No way!" he yells, laughing in her ear. He rolls her

over so she gets covered in the dirty rainwater too. She pulls out of concentration mode, realizes what's happening. He lies on her, mud on his face and dripping from his hair. His clothes are drenched. He holds her down until he realizes she's not struggling to move, just to breathe, and then he eases off. She just looks at him, panting, like she doesn't know what happened. Her breath comes in rasps. "Did I score?"

"Uh . . ." He laughs. "No. Not even close. Are you okay?" he asks. He pushes her filthy hair out of her face, and his face grows concerned. "Hey." His fingers are cold on her cheek.

She heaves and tries to catch her breath. "I think I'm going to puke."

"No, you're not."

"How would you know?"

"I just know. You're fine." He rolls away from her just in case.

"I might drown first."

"Distinct possibility."

They lie gasping, rain pouring over them. Once Kendall can move, she struggles to an upright position. She looks at Jacián in his T-shirt and shorts, totally mud covered. "You must be freezing," she says.

"Yeah." He sits up too, and she can see goose bumps on his arms and legs. "You?"

"I think my sweatshirt weighs fifty pounds. It's keeping me warm just by being so heavy."

"I think I still have Arizona blood." He pulls his knees up. "Not used to this cold."

"Just wait. It'll snow soon. Just like that it'll go from the decent fall weather, pretty colors, to snow. It's probably snowing up in the mountains right now if we're getting rain here."

Jacián gets to his feet. His clothes drip. "Do you ever ride?"

"Sure. We don't have any horses right now."

"I bet I know where you can borrow one."

Kendall smiles and gets up too. They walk to the porch together. "You should get inside. You want me to drip-dry out here? I can call my mom for a ride. I doubt they're out in the fields when it's like this."

"Either way, you won't be welcome in any vehicle like that. You can just take a shower here. We have enough bathrooms. Is that weird?"

"A little. I didn't even think to bring a towel to sit on like I usually do when we play games in the rain."

"It's okay. Seriously."

Kendall feels the chill working into her system too, now. "Okay. Yeah. Thanks." Gingerly she pulls her sodden sweatshirt up over her head and drops it like a rock to the porch. "I'll need a plastic bag for my clothes."

"No problem." He takes off his shoes, peels off his socks, and squeezes out the hems of his shirt and shorts, trying to get as much water out of them as possible so he doesn't drip all over the house. "You remember where Marlena's bathroom is upstairs? 'Cause you're going to have to make a mad dash."

"Yep." She does the same with her clothes and footgear. Thanks to the sweatshirt, her shirt is only wet, not soaked, but it's still sticking to her. When Jacián glances at it, she blushes. "Okay, I'm going to make a run for it."

"Don't forget to bring your clean clothes with you, or you could have another problem," he teases.

Kendall's face turns hot. "Good point." She opens the door and runs nimbly through the house, grabbing her backpack as she goes, and then dashing up the stairs.

A shower never felt so good. Even being alone in the house with Jacián, knowing he's naked in another shower somewhere nearby, doesn't mess with her brain. "Thank you, soccer," she says reverently. She feels terrific. It's been too long. She lathers up and thinks about how much better she feels now than she has since . . . well, since the last time she played soccer with Jacián.

"I wonder if I could get him to dance," she muses out loud as she runs her fingers through her wet hair, trying to comb it.

* * *

She emerges, hair still wet, back in her school clothes, and it feels awkward now. She wonders what she'll find when she gets back downstairs. She creeps down and hears something in the kitchen. She slips into the room and sees Jacián standing at the counter in jeans and with a towel around his neck.

There's no denying the guy works out. He's listening to a message on the answering machine from Mrs. Obregon, saying they're staying in Bozeman for dinner and not to wait to eat. He deletes it.

"Hey," Kendall says.

He reaches into the refrigerator and pulls out two Granny Smith apples and a hunk of cheese. "You hungry? I'm starving."

"Yeah, sure."

He pulls a jar of peanut butter from the cupboard and a knife from the drawer and starts slicing apples.

"I should probably get home soon . . . ," Kendall says. "I'm sure you have stuff to do." She can't stop looking at his chest.

He pauses in his cutting. "You need to go now? I'll drive you."

"No! I mean, no hurry. And not unless you want to. I can call my mom."

"It's okay. I want to." He continues slicing and moves on to the second apple, and then opens the block of cheese and slices that. Hands her a plate. "Here. Apple. Peanut butter. Manchego. Take your pick."

She takes some of each. "So, ah, I'm not sure if you know this, but you're not wearing a shirt."

"Distracting, isn't it?"

"You're pretty sure you're hot, aren't you." It feels more comfortable when they are at odds, somehow.

"You said it."

"And I'm sure I'll regret it. Do you always walk around like that?"

"Yeah, always. You mean this is the first time you noticed?" He drags an apple slice through a glob of peanut butter and takes a bite. "No. Just on laundry day. I'm out of shirts."

"Oh! Crap. Laundry. I need a plastic bag." Kendall jumps off her bar stool. "I left my wet stuff hanging in the shower."

Jacián reaches for a drawer and pulls out a trash bag. "Here."

"Be right back."

She returns moments later to find all the food gone. "Wow."

"I was really hungry."

"Apparently."

He grins. "I'm a growing boy. What do you want from me?"

"I don't know, maybe the rest of the food that was on *my plate*?"

"Dude, you left."

"Next time I'll take my plate with me."

"Next time." He raises an eyebrow. "Tomorrow?"

She looks at him. So conflicted. She knows her parents could use her help, but harvest is almost done. And if she begs off, she knows her mother will say yes. After the relief her brain is experiencing right now, she wants to get back out there and continue playing until she collapses.

And then there's just one more nagging feeling. One that she pushes back every time she has a pleasant conversation with Jacián. She knows it's stupid. But when she thinks about how much Nico might have suffered, or might be suffering. . . . How can she do anything fun—especially with another guy—and feel good about it?

It just feels wrong.

"I didn't know it was such a loaded question." Jacián is leaning on the counter now, looking at Kendall intently during her silence.

She swallows hard. "It's not. It's . . . I don't know. I'll have to see."

Jacián nods. "Okay." He goes into the adjacent laundry room and comes out wearing a Phoenix Suns sweatshirt.

"My dad's a big fan," he explains, rolling his eyes. "You ready?" he asks. He pulls his truck keys from his pocket.

Kendall nods.

He drives her home in silence. When he gets to her driveway, he says, "You know, if you ever want to talk about it, I . . . I could listen. Or, you know. Whatever."

"Thanks. I don't know if . . ." She grabs her backpack, which weighs a ton because of the wet clothes. "Thanks," she says again. And because of his sincerity, she reaches over and squeezes his hand. And then she slips out of the truck and doesn't look back.

That night Kendall sleeps hard and soundly for the first time since Nico disappeared.

WE

ANGER. Again We are stalled, turned back from Our plan. Our souls pound and rock the metal, the wood, the room, and the building. Revenge is near. Thirty-five. One hundred. Thirty-five. One hundred! In agony, We scrape a new message.

Touch me.
Tell no one.
It's me.

TWENTY

The sun shines again. It's Friday, and Nico's desk is still in its place.

She almost doesn't notice it—the words.

But she does. How could she not?

There's nothing else she can do. She brushes it with her fingertips when she passes the desk to sharpen her pencil. And again when she throws something in the trash. And she hears it, barely. The whisper. Nico's voice. *Touch me. Tell no one. It's me.*

At lunch she waits until everyone is outside, and then she moves to it. Cautiously she slips her fingers over the new graffiti, back and forth, as Nico's voice fills her ears.

Her heart pounds. How can this be happening?

She rests her cheek against it, closes her eyes, and absorbs his words. It's not as strong, not as overpowering this time. It starts out gentle and builds, hovers, the euphoria that comes over her.

By the time lunch is over, Kendall doesn't want to pull away. She stays where she is, unmoving, not listening to Ms. Hinkler, not caring what anybody else in the class might think about her unauthorized move. Not noticing the puzzled looks from Jacián and Eli and the others. Nothing matters but the words and the solace they bring.

When Jacián and Marlena nudge her at the end of the day, Kendall pulls herself away. It's like the afternoon was only minutes long. And now she has to leave him, leave Nico, for the entire weekend. The incredible high drains slowly, and by the time the three of them are at Hector's, Kendall feels like she just came off of a very big sugar rush. She's lethargic and her brain is muddled.

"What's up with you today?" Jacián asks as they stretch for soccer. Marlena sits wrapped up in a blanket on the porch, watching, her foot propped up on the railing.

"Nothing much," Kendall says. Her voice sounds far away.

"You got tired of sitting by me?"

"Huh? No. I just . . ." She trails off, wondering what she's going to say. "I just feel closer to Nico when I'm sitting there."

Jacián grabs a ball and starts dribbling. He doesn't say anything.

Kendall goes through the motions of doing some exercises but when Jacián passes the ball to her, she misses, or doesn't make the effort to return the ball.

"Come on," he mutters.

Kendall shakes her arms and does a quick jog in place in an attempt to clear her head. "Sorry. I'm not sure . . ." She tries to concentrate, and slowly, as she focuses and puts some effort into the sport, the fuzziness in her brain clears. By the time she's fully into playing, questions start bombarding. As she runs, the questions sound out at every step.

What is happening to me?

How is it possible?

Is this what Nico was feeling when he was so distant, those days before he disappeared?

She stops short and lets Jacián steal the ball as she realizes how strange everything was today. "Oh my God," she says in a strange voice. "Oh my God. I'm going insane." She flops to the grass, her head pounding, as Jacián comes running over.

"Are you okay?" he asks.

Kendall looks up at him for a long moment. She shakes

her head no. And then she bursts into tears. "Something is happening to me!" she sobs.

Jacián drops to the ground next to her, facing her. He reaches out, and she clings to him, burying her face and crying into his neck. He holds her, pats her back, pushes her hair from her face and whispers in her ear. "It's okay, Kendall. It's okay."

"Something weird is happening!" she cries again. "I don't want to disappear. I thought I might want to . . . to be with him, but I don't. I don't want to. I'm so scared."

Jacián smoothes his hand over Kendall's hair. "Nobody else wants you to either," he says.

Marlena, on the porch, hops up on her good foot to get a better look at what's happening. Jacián waves her off. She scowls and then retreats inside the house to watch from the window.

"I'm so scared," Kendall says again, a whisper this time.

"Tell me why," Jacián says. "Do you know something? Did something happen?" He pulls away and looks at her. Wipes the tears from her cheeks with gentle fingers.

Kendall thinks for a long moment, trying to decide. Knowing anything she says about the desk will sound completely loony. "It's crazy. I'm going crazy. I swear. I can't tell you why. I—I don't even know why."

"What can I do to help you?" Jacián asks. His eyes are filled with concern. There is nothing left of his hardness, his anger from when Kendall first met him.

She can't tell him. "I just . . ." She bites her lip and then tries to laugh at her own ridiculousness. Because, thinking back on the day, it all seems so crazy. Like she was hypnotized or something. And now it's like she has snapped out of it. Like it's probably all just her imagination. "I just need to stop thinking about Nico for a while, I think. Not forget him, just . . . try to let him go a little bit."

Jacián swallows hard and looks off into the woods for a moment, like he doesn't know what to say. Then he nods. "Okay . . . um . . ."

"Yeah. So. Can you help me?" She sniffs and wipes her eyes. "Sorry about all the crying."

"Sure. And I don't mind. Once in a while, I mean." He laughs. "I don't get what I can do to help you, though. Keep you occupied? Like, maybe you and I could go riding tomorrow."

"Yeah, like that. That sounds good. I'm going to tell my parents that I need to have some time away from all that thinking that happens when I'm working on the farm. They'll let me. They're worried."

"And Sunday, you're coming for Marlena's birthday party?"

"Yes," Kendall says. "Yes. Thank you. Okay." She sighs in relief. "That sounds good. I hope you don't get sick of me. You're a real champ to do this."

"Well, it's a hardship, that's for sure. Just looking at you makes me want to go and . . . do something."

"Ooh, zinger."

"Yeah, pathetic. I'll work on that."

Kendall hops to her feet, a little embarrassed and ready to end this episode of the ongoing drama. "Okay," she says. "Ready to finish this game?" She offers a hand.

"The rules say the game's not over until you assault me with a flagrant foul, you know."

"Hey, it wasn't flagrant." She slaps his head.

Jacián grabs her hand and gets up. "Yesterday? Grabbing me around the waist and tripping me? No, that was really subtle, Fletcher. No call. Now," he says lightly, though his eyes pierce through her, "let's see if you can keep your hands off me." He draws his thumb across her jaw, catching a lingering teardrop.

An unexpected longing pierces her gut, runs through her whole body, and her lips part in surprise. "No problem," she says. Not quite sure she means it.

WE

We had you. For a moment We had you wrapped inside Our core. You were a cricket in Our web.

Our patience is thin, Our souls shellacked in wood. We need you.

Come back, little cricket.

SAVE ME!
I'M ALIVE.
SAY YES.

TWENTY-ONE

Saturday dawns clear. At breakfast Kendall thinks about school and the desk, and knows it has to be her mind messing with her. Playing tricks. It's the stress, she knows. Hanging around with Jacián and being normal? It sounds awesome. Riding again? Fantastic. It's been months.

"You're off the job for the rest of the season," her father says. "Do you need to visit your shrink again?"

"Nathan," Mrs. Fletcher chides.

"Sorry. Your psychologist?"

"I don't care if you call her a shrink," Kendall says, mouth full of pancakes. "And no, I think I'm okay. I just need to do some of the old techniques again to control this OCD. I know what to do. It's just all the time I have to think about

Nico in school, and then in the fields . . . it was really getting to me. Making me a little bit crazy." A lot crazy, to be honest.

"I told you, Nathan," Mrs. Fletcher says. "This kind of schedule for her was a bad idea, after everything that's happened."

"Hey!" Mr. Fletcher says. "Why is everything suddenly all my fault?"

"And then the rejection from Juilliard . . ."

"Yeah, thanks for the reminder," Kendall says. The mention of Juilliard, the lack of future plans, dampens her mood considerably.

"Sorry," Mrs. Fletcher says, "but it's true you need to start thinking about another option sometime soon."

"But, Mother!" Kendall flops her head onto the table. She knows it's true.

"Now, where are you going to be today?"

Kendall lifts her head. "I'm going riding."

"With?"

"With . . . Jacián." She feels guilty saying it. As if maybe Nico is somewhere listening.

"Is Marlena going too?"

"No," she says wryly, "she's not quite ready to get back on the horse."

Mr. Fletcher snickers.

Mrs. Fletcher looks concerned. "Does he know how to ride?"

"Yeah. Marlena said they had horses in Arizona. And he rides Hector's now and then."

"You stay close to town, okay? Don't go too far." Mrs. Fletcher's voice is nervous.

"Mother, may I remind you that when the two individuals disappeared, they were in town? We're probably safer the farther out we ride."

"I know. I just worry."

"We'll be fine. Back by dark."

"Fine. Call me if you need a ride, though I'll be out working until sundown."

Mr. Fletcher drains the last of his coffee and shoves his chair back wearily, ready for another day. "Should be done by week's end," he says.

Mrs. Fletcher follows him but stops to give Kendall a peck on the cheek. "Have fun. You could use some fun for once."

"I will. See you tonight. I'll call when we're back at the ranch. You and Daddy are going to Hector's for dinner tomorrow, right? Did he call?"

"Yes, he called. We're going to try. We lost most of two days this week because of the rain, you know . . . but Dad and I could use a break too."

"Cool." Kendall reaches out and hugs her mother. "Thanks for letting me off work," she says.

* * *

When Jacián comes to pick her up, Kendall has a backpack filled with water and food, an emergency kit, and a blanket to sit on for lunch. She's wearing jeans and boots and grabs her jacket and a cowboy hat on the way out.

"You get your deliveries done already?" she asks as they head back to the ranch.

"I did them last night and two this morning. Done."

"Sweet."

Back at Hector's they walk out to the horse barn. Marlena waves forlornly from the window. "She's pathetic," Jacián says.

"I feel bad she can't do anything."

"She's got friends coming over. She'll be fine. Plus, she gets a big blowout party tomorrow."

"True."

The barn is quiet, eerie. They saddle up two quarter horses and lead them out. Kendall unpacks her backpack and leaves it inside the barn, loads the saddlebags with the goods, and then mounts. They head off on a path toward the woods at a brisk walk, quiet at first. It smells crisp and piney.

After a while Kendall's mind starts running circles around her, about the desk and Nico. Trying to forget about all of that, she asks, "Remember when you were in my driveway?"

"Yeah."

"You told me the next day that you were feeling bad about something so you were out for a walk. What was going on?"

"Oh." Jacián seems surprised by the question. "Um . . . yeah. No big deal."

"Come on. What?"

"Well, it's been kind of hard moving here. I think it was the full moon or something that had me down—I'm fine."

"You're so tough." She rolls her eyes.

"Yeah, maybe."

Kendall shrugs. "Let me guess. You left your girlfriend back in Arizona, you hate the outdoors, miss the city, are forced to spend your last year of high school with a bunch of strangers and to do all kinds of crap work involving animal dung, for a grandfather you barely know. You leave your big city high school soccer team behind for a rinky-dink cowboy half team full of hicks, and then the season gets canceled because one too many players disappear without a trace. How'm I doing?"

Jacián smiles in spite of himself. "You're pretty much batting a thousand so far."

"And then you have no chance at a scholarship because you can't show a scout your amazing moves."

"True . . ."

"You make it sound like there's more."

"Well, there's being accused of kidnapping upon first moving to an all-white town."

"It's not all white. Old Mr. Greenwood is pure Blackfeet Tribe, according to Eli. There are others of different races. Travis's mom is Cambodian."

"All right, whatever. That part's over."

"Plus, nobody thinks you did anything now. They were happy to pin the blame on Nico just as soon as he was unable to speak for himself."

Jacián is quiet for a moment. The horses lean forward as they ascend a small hill. "I don't think he did anything."

"It's weird, though, right?"

"Yeah. What do you think happened?"

Kendall thinks about the desk. About how strange Nico acted. About how she felt like she was in a trance yesterday when she sat there. About the coincidence of Nico and Tiffany both sitting at that desk, and about how Nico's car was at school when he disappeared.

"Kendall? You okay?"

Kendall glances at him. "If I tell you something weird, will you think I'm . . . like . . . weird?"

"Probably." He smiles to let her know he's teasing.

"You know Tiffany Quinn, the girl who disappeared in May? Both she and Nico had the same desk."

Jacián is quiet.

"It's just a coincidence. I mean, who would even know that except for stupid OCD me."

"Yeah," Jacián says slowly. "That is a weird coincidence." He looks at Kendall, eyebrows furrowed. Thinking. But he says nothing more.

"You think I'm weird."

"You are weird. But that's not a bad thing."

They travel onward to a huge open field, cattle roaming wild. "Are these some of yours?" Kendall asks.

Jacián rides close to check the brand. "Looks that way."

"Who gets to round them up when winter hits?"

"My parents. Me. Maybe Marlena if she's allowed on a quad again soon."

"Does Hector ride still?"

"Not four-wheelers. But horses? Sure. He'll never give that up."

"I haven't seen him on a horse in a while. How's his health?"

"He's just taking it easy. Finally semiretired, now that my parents are here. He spends a lot of time with old Mr. Greenwood."

Kendall thinks. "He said they've been friends since they were teenagers."

Jacián nods. "They both got sent to the same reform school."

"What?" Kendall pulls up on her horse. "Are you serious?"

"Totally serious. He told me the other day."

"Around here?"

"Not far. Just a few miles away. There's an overgrown gravel driveway if you take the viaduct all the way around north to nowhere. You'd miss it if you didn't know it was there. When we were out searching for Nico," he says, "we got near to the back end of the reform school's property, which is actually a lot closer to the ranch as the crow flies but totally inaccessible. The school got shut down a long time ago. Abandoned. It's all completely overgrown now. Grandfather didn't want to go anywhere near it."

"Why?"

"He said it was a bad place. He didn't want to talk about it. Said he'd never go back again. Too many memories."

"Poor Hector. He's so nice."

"Too bad none of it rubbed off on me, huh?" Jacián grins.

Kendall laughs. "That's pretty much what I used to think about you! You know, you really pissed me off when you told me I was putting the meat in the freezer wrong. I wanted to punch you."

"I was quite aware of that. However, you have to cut me some slack. I didn't know about your little . . . uh . . .

special gift back then. You do realize that the way you were stacking them was totally not logical, right?"

"Sure, I know that, but why the hell did you care? Are you some kind of control freak?"

"Maybe a little. Not much anymore. I gave it up." He laughs bitterly. "It's clear I have no control over anything these days."

They are quiet for a while. The trail meanders in front of them, leading to a wide-open space. Jacián clucks his tongue and leans forward. His horse trots, then canters. Kendall flies after him, and they have a good chase for a quarter of an hour to where the woods grow thick.

"That was awesome," Kendall says. Her cheeks glow. They dismount, and Kendall rummages around, finding the things she packed for lunch. "This day rocks. Thanks for making me go."

Jacián stretches out on his back on the blanket. He plucks a long wheatlike weed and chews on it. "Yeah, I really had to twist your arm."

Kendall plops down beside him. "Oh, stop it. Why do we always have to argue?"

"Because it's fun?"

Kendall smacks his chest, but this time he is ready. He grabs her arm and holds it tightly to his chest, pulls her toward him. "Don't."

Kendall struggles one-armed to sit up, surprise on her

face. "Don't what?" She can feel his body heat through his shirt.

"I think you're afraid to like me." Jacián's dark eyes slice into hers for a long moment before he speaks again. "If you want to touch me, Kendall, then touch me. Don't hide behind those little girl slaps."

Her eyes widen, and she stares at him as something stirs in the pit of her gut. Something incredible. And a little scary. Something she's never felt before. But all she can say is, "What makes you think I want to touch you? I have a boyfriend. You have a girlfriend."

"Is that the way it is?"

Kendall swallows hard. "Seems pretty clear that it is."

Jacián holds her arm a moment longer, a flicker in his eyes and at the corner of his mouth the only indications he heard her. And then he releases her. "Whatever." He clears his throat and gets to his feet, then pulls apples and some grain from his saddlebag for the horses.

Kendall stares at him from the blanket. Then she shakes her head and opens up her lunch, sorting her fruit salad into sections of the bowl before eating. But she tastes nothing. Her mouth is like sawdust. Because she knows one thing is true, even though she hasn't wanted to admit it.

The missing boyfriend who would do anything for her, who has been her best friend since birth? Never. Ever. Made her feel like that. Never made her gut twist just with a look, a touch. Never made her so hot she wanted to tackle him, kiss him hard. Press her body against his and roll around in a field, not even caring that little bits of grass were getting on her clothes.

"You're not going to eat?" she says after a while, breaking the awkward silence.

"I'm not hungry."

"I made you a lunch."

"Thanks. But I'm still not hungry."

Kendall glares. How can somebody be so hot one minute and so annoying the next? Whatever the case, the perfect day is ruined.

Ruined by the truth.

And the guilt builds. The guilt of Nico. She curses her own weakness. He's only been missing a month. It's no different from if she'd gone to Juilliard and he'd gone to Bozeman.

Except it is. It's vastly different. Worse, because he no longer has a voice. Worse, because what would people say if she gave up on him? What would Nico's parents say? What if he's *not* dead? She imagines the looks on their faces.

And on his.

"Stop it," she mutters. She can't let her brain go to weird places. Nothing happened. And nothing will.

* * *

The silence grows prickly and painful as they pack up. Head home.

She starts counting horse steps anxiously as they travel back to the ranch. One hundred, five hundred. Even when she hits a thousand, she can't stop counting. She can't stop, she decides, until she hears a hawk cry.

After two thousand she convinces herself that if she hears either a mourning dove or a hawk she can end this. At three thousand she concludes that if she sees a grouse or even a goddamn rabbit, she can stop counting. Finally, thankfully, at 3,842 the rabbit comes through for her.

But the rabbit doesn't fix her problem.

So the counting begins again, fresh from zero.

Her anxiety builds. She hates this. Just wants to go home.

They put the horses in the barn, and Kendall watches awkwardly as Jacián tends to them, rubbing them down, getting them water and food, putting their blankets on them. He doesn't look at her. Eventually she just turns and leaves, walking up to the house alone. She knocks on the door and is greeted by Mrs. Obregon and a delicious smell and sizzle from the stove. Her stomach, after only the few pieces of fruit for lunch, growls loudly.

"Can you stay for dinner?" Mrs. Obregon asks, handing Kendall the phone.

"Yes," Marlena says. "Stay!"

"I should get home." Kendall dials her mother and prays for her to pick up. But there's no answer. "Hey, Mom," she says to the machine, thinking fast. "I'm back at Hector's. Yeah. Mmm-hmm. It was good. Just pick me up . . . whenever. . . ." She trails off. "Okay. See you soon. Bye."

Kendall hangs up the phone and smiles with a brightness she doesn't feel. "My mom'll be here in a minute. I'm going to wait outside. Thanks for . . . yeah. The horses. Everything."

Kendall turns as Marlena and Mrs. Obregon watch her, puzzled looks on their faces.

As darkness falls, Kendall slips through the trees and runs.

She doesn't see Jacián standing in the driveway, watching her go.

Doesn't know it's him driving by late that night when she stands in front of the upstairs window, crying for Nico to forgive her.

WE

Alone again, so long. This time We wait. This time We know for sure. That heat, that heartbeat, that life—will be back.

I need you.

TWENTY-TWO

All night Kendall dreams about the desk and Nico. She sleeps in on Sunday but wakes with a start and wonders, what if . . . wherever Nico is, he's trying to send her a message? What if it's not her imagination or her grief or her OCD, but it's real?

She sits up, disoriented, bright sunshine streaming into her bedroom.

What if Nico's really able, somehow, to connect with her? And all this time she's been ignoring his calls for help?

By the time she hits the shower, she's laughing it off again. "Fletcher," she says, "get a fricking grip, will you?" As she dresses, she's wondering if maybe she does need to see the shrink again. It's not that she doesn't like her doctor. She's really been helpful through all the tough times. But it makes Kendall feel sort of like she's backsliding. Which, just maybe, she is. "It probably wouldn't hurt to see her once," she mutters.

Alone in the house, Kendall nibbles at a muffin and wraps the present she bought for Marlena from the general store—a set of earrings with little topaz stones. And then, because she's bored, she makes cookies, thinking it might be good to bring something to the party.

By two Kendall is flipping through channels on TV, watching televangelists, infomercials, and cartoons. She goes out back to see if her mother and father are coming, but she sees no one except stupid Brandon's father, who is helping out on weekends with harvest. She heads back inside and waits some more.

She's sure they forgot.

At two forty-five, the phone rings.

"Hello?"

"Where are you?" It's Marlena with a pouty voice.

"I'm waiting for my douchey parents to get here so they can drive me. I think they forgot." She hears music and laughing in the background.

"Why didn't you call? Jacián will come get you. Jacián!" She yells into the phone. "Go pick up Kendall!"

"No, that's okay—"

"He's on the way. Just get here!"

Kendall hangs up and sighs. Writes a note to her parents. Grabs her coat, the gift, and the cookies and goes outside to wait on the front steps.

"Thanks," Kendall says, getting into the truck. "Sorry."

Jacián, clad in an apron and smelling like smoke, waves her off and speeds back toward Hector's.

Kendall grips the armrest. "You trying to get a speeding ticket?"

Jacián shrugs. "Sheriff is at my house having margaritas and carne asada, and my poblanos are probably burning."

"You cook, too?"

"No. I grill. I don't know how to cook." He flies up the driveway, parks next to a row of vehicles, and exits the truck almost before the engine quits. Runs for the smoke-filled backyard to an open fire pit with a big grate on it. He grabs a pair of tongs and starts flipping charred-looking things over.

Kendall watches him for a minute, then walks into the house and greets Marlena with a hug. Eli, Travis, and stupid Brandon are there, as well as some juniors and the group of sophomore girls that Marlena has become friends with. Everybody mingles loudly, all varieties of Latin music playing in the background. At least a quarter of Cryer's Cross is here. Mrs. Obregon works the blender, making drinks for the adult guests, and Hector serves up sodas for the under-twenty-one crowd.

Kendall grabs a Dr Pepper and weaves through the people, observing. Lots of parents are here. Even Nico's parents. Kendall feels guilty that she hasn't been by to see them lately. She walks over to say hello. They look terrible.

"Hey, Mr. and Mrs. Cruz," she says.

"Hi, Kendall, sweetheart," Mrs. Cruz says. She gives her a long hug. "Are your parents here?"

"No, not yet. I guess they had to finish up some stuff on the farm." Kendall can't help but stare at the bags under Mrs. Cruz's eyes. "How are you doing?"

She smiles and shrugs, eyes glistening. "You can imagine, I'm sure."

Kendall nods, and they stand there, awkwardly looking around the room, nothing else to say. "It was great of you to come."

Mr. Cruz nods. He looks grayer than ever. "We needed to get out. It was nice to be invited." He stares off. "I think I'll go help Mr. Obregon with . . . whatever he needs help with."

"And I promised Carmelita I'd help with serving," Mrs. Cruz says. "Good seeing you, Kendall."

Kendall smiles a tight smile and nods. "Yeah, you too."

From behind Kendall comes a voice. "That was awkward."

Kendall turns and sees Eli Greenwood. She sighs with relief. "Yeah . . . It's so weird now. It's like I don't know what to say to them."

"It's the same with Tiffany's parents."

"Oh no. Are they here too?"

"No. They said they couldn't make it."

"This has to be a hard thing to attend. I'm surprised the Cruzes came. Seeing all of us here . . ."

"Yeah, it's weird."

They take in the crowd for a moment before Kendall's eyes stray to the backyard. She watches Jacián at the fire pit. He's flipping a tortilla in a small cast-iron skillet now. "So, how's the food?"

"It's pretty awesome. You need to get some. Here, I'll help you." He grins. "Get another plate for myself while I'm at it."

They load up their plates full of food and snake their way outside to the deck, where there's room to eat and it's not so noisy. Hector is outside now too, sitting with Eli's grandfather. Marlena and the group of sophomore girls stand a dozen feet away, eating, gossiping. Several of them are watching Jacián lustily, and Kendall feels a ridiculous pang of jealousy. She shoves a soft taco into her mouth and glares.

"So, your brother," one of the girls says to Marlena. The others giggle.

"What about him?"

"He's so broody and cute."

"He's got a girlfriend," one of the others says. "Get over it."

Marlena chews wildly and waves at her mouth as if that will make the food go away. She swallows and says, "Nope. He's single. He broke up with his girlfriend last week."

The girls gasp loudly enough to make Jacián look. When they break into giggles, he scowls and turns his back again.

Kendall's jaw drops. She wonders why he didn't mention that yesterday on the little ride that turned weird. She's not sure how that makes her feel.

Eli rolls his eyes. "Dammit," he says. "That guy is not making things easier around here."

Kendall slips an arm around her friend's waist. "Aw, don't worry, honey," she says. "They'll get over him eventually, and then you can swoop in and attack."

Eli laughs. "I've done enough swooping. I think I'm going to have to look elsewhere. Too many guys, not enough girls around here." He shrugs. "Where are you going to college? Do you know yet?"

Kendall sighs. "No. I don't know. I might just hang around here."

"Don't be stupid, Kendall."

"What? Why?"

"You're really smart and talented. Get the heck out of here."

"But what if . . ."

Eli looks at her. "What if what? What if Nico comes back and you're not here? Look . . . it's really hard to say this to you because I know it hurts, but you know that it's not likely. The chances we'll ever see him again . . . Well, you know the statistics. And even if he does come back, there are lots of ways of finding you to let you know. Maybe you can even get a cell phone once you get out of here."

Kendall sets her plate on the deck railing. It hurts to hear what he's saying, but she knows it's true. The thoughts start whipping through her brain again. "So," she says, trying to fight them off, "where are you going to college?"

"Vassar."

"Seriously?"

"Yeah. Tons of women there."

Kendall laughs. "Good for you. You got accepted?"

"Yep." Eli looks at his feet and blushes. "Got the letter the other day."

"That is so cool!" She hugs him tightly. "I'm really glad for you."

"Thanks. Want to make out?"

Kendall laughs. "No, not since that unfortunate spin the bottle incident in sixth grade in stupid Brandon's basement."

"Yeah, I thought you'd say that. But hey, worth a try." Eli scoops the last bit of salsa from his plate and licks his fingers. "Now for dessert," he says. "I heard there's flan. And cookies." He winks at her.

"Go for it." Kendall smiles as she watches Eli go back inside, and then she turns back to her plate. She glances at Jacián again, and this time he's staring intently at her. When he sees her looking, he turns away and roughly shoves charred peppers into a paper bag.

She puts her fork down, suddenly not hungry anymore, and then turns to bring her plate inside.

Inside, people are dancing. Marlena's still using crutches with her boot, so dancing is out of the question for her. Kendall hangs out on the couch with her and the other girls for a while, but then with a little encouragement, she joins in.

Her adrenaline soars. It feels so good to dance after weeks without it. As the afternoon progresses into evening, the half-drunk adults completely clear the living room of furniture and really start the celebration.

Kendall dances with Hector and with Eli, even though he's terrible at it and keeps stepping on her feet. She gets lots of cheers from the partyers. It's so much fun—she wonders why the little town doesn't do parties more often. Stupid potatoes.

As it grows late, more people drop out or leave

entirely, but Marlena shouts for Kendall to stay, to keep dancing. The other girls get up on the floor with her, and things get a little wild. When one of them spins and trips, Hector turns on a sexy couples song to clear away the singles. It's perfect for the salsa.

Hector has bowed out of the dancing portion, claiming he's too old and tired, and none of the boys have a clue how to do it. So Kendall steps to the doorway and watches Mr. and Mrs. Obregon dance. A few other couples join in, but there aren't many in this town who know the steps.

A moment later Jacián appears inside the house for the first time since the party started. He's wearing a fresh white T-shirt. He steps into the room and goes up to his parents. "Hey, Mama!" he shouts, a smile on his face. She laughs and waves at him to come. Jacián cuts in on his father, taking his mother by the hand.

The girls in the room go slack-jawed as he moves almost perfectly to the gorgeous dance. When he messes up, he grins wide, and his mother smiles back.

Kendall stares.

Mr. Obregon stands next to her. "He's not bad, my boy," he says proudly. Mr. Obregon has a deep accent, deeper than and different from Hector's. His voice is rich and warm and just a bit more weathered than Jacián's.

Kendall swallows hard. "How did he learn that?"

"It was a part of his soccer training. All of the soccer,

basketball, and football teams at his old school learn to dance. Makes them better players."

"Impressive," Kendall says. *No wonder he's so fluid on the field*, Kendall thinks. That twinge inside her grows stronger. She feels like she's drooling. And there, across the room, are Nico's parents, watching her. Kendall tears her eyes away from Jacián. She weaves through the group of people crowded at the door and slips out, down the hallway and outside to where she can breathe. She takes one last look at Jacián through the picture window and then walks out into the yard, the chill of evening feeling delicious on her sweaty skin. She walks past the still-smoldering fire pit and heads toward the horse barn, breathing in the scents of fall. Leaves crunch under her feet. She takes in the deep night, the bright stars. The silence of air.

The horse barn is locked up for the night. It figures, considering the strange stuff of Cryer's Cross these days. Kendall sinks to the grass and leans up against the barn wall, staring into the night. Thinking.

About everything. Nico. And college. Jacián and how hot she feels lately when she's around him. And then the guilt comes again. Pounding her, beating her up.

Alongside that is the crazy, otherworldly scariness of the desk. And again, now that she is alone, she wonders if there actually might be something real about it. What if it truly is

Nico? What if he is trapped in the school, being kept tied up by . . . by old Mr. Greenwood? And maybe he is allowed to roam the school at night, leaving messages for Kendall?

But why wouldn't he leave them on Kendall's desk? And if it were Nico doing the graffiti, how could he make the new stuff look like it had been there for years—and why would he want to?

Kendall thinks she knows now. She's pretty damn sure.

Because that desk, the desk that makes people disappear, is possessed.

And maybe so are the people who touch it.

It dawns on her. There's no kidnapper. There's absolutely no need for this crazy buddy system. Kendall could wander Cryer's Cross naked in the middle of the darkest night and nobody would kidnap her.

It's not a who.

It's a what.

She shudders violently. "Fletcher! You're crazy," she reprimands. "Knock it off already."

A stick crackles, as if Kendall's outburst startles someone. Kendall whips around and scrambles to her feet. She peers into the darkness. Her heart pounds. She backs up to the barn as tightly as she can, as if its size and structure can give her strength.

A figure appears and stops abruptly as if it senses her.

Kendall freezes. "Who's there?"

"It's just me," Jacián says. He walks toward her, peering through the darkness. "Your parents are here. They're worried because they couldn't find you."

"Oh."

"I said I knew where you were and that you were fine."

"Oh," she says again. Flustered. "Did you?"

"I saw you go out." He stands there a moment. "So you should probably go back inside and prove that for me now, so I don't get interrogated again. For the third time." He turns and starts walking back to the house.

"Jacián," Kendall says.

"What?"

She jogs to catch up to him, not knowing what she intends to say, only that she doesn't want him to walk away. "You're a really good dancer."

"So are you." His voice is husky from working in the smoke all evening.

"You saw?"

His silence is affirmation enough.

Kendall shoves her hands into her jeans pockets, shivers a little. "When did you break up with your girlfriend?"

He's quiet for a minute. "That night I went to your house. It was over between us months ago, when I moved. It just took us a long time to say it out loud."

"Why didn't you tell me?"

He shoves a hand into his pocket and looks up to the

sky. "It didn't seem like it would make any difference to you." After a moment he turns toward the house and starts walking again, faster this time.

"Jacián," she says again, and jogs after him. "Wait."

"What now?"

"I . . . just . . ." She grips his arm. Feels her heart pound.

He stops. Turns toward her. "You feel like slapping me again?"

"Yes," she says. She can hardly breathe.

He stands there for a moment, and then he slips his fingers behind her neck, weaving them into her hair, his breath warm on her face. He crushes his lips against hers, pulls her body close, closer.

Kendall can't think. She reaches for his neck, his face, tentatively, moving to his chest, grabbing his T-shirt in her fingers. She can't breathe. Doesn't want to breathe. Just wants to forget everything.

Just as abruptly he pulls away. "What do you want, Kendall? Are you really ready for this? I don't think you are."

She gasps and takes a step back. "Shit," she says. "I'm so sorry."

He stares. "Me too."

"You understand that I can't . . ."

He closes his eyes wearily. Takes a deep breath, lets it out, and turns away. "You can't," he says. "You can't do anything because of your missing boyfriend." His voice is filled with bitterness. "Sure, I understand. Yeah, you just wanted to get a freebie, just a little something, so you can keep mourning without missing too much action. What's not to understand? Besides the fact that it was obvious you two were so much more like brother and sister than boyfriend and girlfriend." He doesn't wait for her to respond. "Obvious to me from the moment I saw you."

"You don't know anything," Kendall says.

"Maybe you should think about getting a different ride to school. How about your other boyfriend, Eli?"

"What, now you're you jealous of Eli?" she blurts out. But then she gets control. "His car is full already. And maybe you're right about Nico and me, and I just didn't know any different." She bites her lip, still tasting Jacián, hating herself for wanting to kiss him again. "Jacián," she says quietly. "All I know is that Nico never made me feel like you make me feel. Nobody does."

Jacián stands there a long moment, agonizing, and then rips his fingers through his hair and turns back toward the horse barn. "God, Kendall! Don't. I can't do this." He swallows hard and looks away. "You do this, and I'm the one who looks bad." His eyes bite through the darkness, but his voice is resigned. "I can't keep being the bad guy around here."

He turns away and jogs off into the darkness.

Kendall trudges slowly, numbly, to the house.

WE

We slumber, lying in wait, saving Our strength for the day. Now sensing, now quivering. Thirty-five, one hundred. Thirty-five, one hundred.

Redemption dawns.

TWENTY-THREE

Kendall goes to sleep thinking about Jacián, but at night her dreams are about Nico again, urgently trying to contact her through the desk. He pleads, cries out, begging her to find him, save him.

When she wakes up, sluggish and still exhausted, her heart is all mixed up about how she's supposed to be feeling about guys and life and death. So conflicted. But the one thing that's clear to Kendall is that she needs to go back there. Back to Nico's desk one more time. Because if she doesn't, she'll never shake the feeling that his blood is on her hands, that she could save him if she just weren't so stubborn.

The ride to school is quiet. Marlena, in the middle with a birthday-cake hangover, rests her head against the seat back and whines about how tired she is. Jacián drives stone-faced. Kendall aches. They are all lacking sleep for a variety of reasons.

Kendall knows that whatever happened last night, it's never going to happen again. She's devoted to Nico. She has to be. No matter what. At least until somebody knows something about what happened to him. She moves mechanically.

Jacián doesn't speak to Kendall. Resolute, she goes about her morning routine and then, as if drawn in, she forgoes the pretense of starting at her own desk, and just sits at Nico's.

She sees the new graffiti and is only mildly surprised. Recklessly she dives into that world, no resistance this time. She drinks in the words, running her fingers over them, hearing Nico's voice calling to her. She rests her cheek on the desk, facing away from Jacián. Her throat catches when she hears Nico's voice lingering over the short phrases.

Save me. I'm alive.

Say yes. I need you.

Come back.

"I'm back," she whispers. "I'm here." Not caring. Never caring again. "Yes, Nico." Slowly she feels something fill her body, fill the emptiness inside.

Throughout the morning Nico's voice grows stronger, more desperate. Over and over he begs Kendall to save him, to come to him, and she can't pull herself away.

Not that she wants to. She is forever in that moment just before sleep, that sweet hovering of a moment where nothing else matters. Sounds, urges, all is deep background noise. This, she realizes . . . this is truly where her brain doesn't rule her world.

As Kendall floats to the sound of Nico's voice for hours, something changes. His voice, it grows increasingly urgent, deeper, darker—like it's inside her. Part of her now. Over time she realizes that the voice doesn't really even sound like Nico at all anymore. And another layer chimes in, like in a round, chanting, *Thirty-five, one hundred. Thirty-five, one hundred.* But really, it doesn't matter anymore in this floating world. She is trapped here. And she doesn't mind.

Then the words change.

Beneath her cheek, swirling in whispers through her body. The words become cold and restless. Strong. Powerful.

Come to me.
Tonight.
Tell no one!
Only you can save me.

Thirty-five, one hundred. Kendall shudders in her surreal state. It's as if all the warmth is sucked from the room.

Still, she is caught there, alone except for the new, strange voice. She's trapped by the mesmerizing feeling, the seductive timbre. She floats, shivering, the cold coming from within, and she is unable to snap out of it on her own. Unable to care enough to try. She is one with the voice.

She knows how it will be. She can see it now. There are pictures flashing behind her eyes—gravel road, long grasses, tangled vines, a fence—hints of where she must go. She accepts it. Accepts her fate as the one who must sacrifice something so that she can save Nico.

And they shall have her. Their way. It is the right way.

When Kendall shakes her at the end of the school day, she rises, sluggish, to her feet, takes her things.

"Are you okay?" Marlena asks.

Jacián fails at his attempt to ignore Kendall completely.

"I'm just so tired," Kendall says, slurring her words. And she is. It feels like she hasn't slept in a week. Yet she is aware enough to know that she has only one task on which to focus. One goal before it's all over. One rule—that she must return tonight to save him. And tell no one.

Or Nico will die.

At her request Jacián and Marlena drop Kendall off at home. She trudges up to her bedroom and collapses onto the bed to daydream about seeing Nico again.

She pictures it, as if the desk is inside her, feeding her still. The back of her school, where she can enter through the always unlocked cellar door. And the place where Nico is—dark and spooky, fog rolling. Massive trees and overgrown brush too thick to pass through. An iron gate, rusty underneath miles of coiled, creeping vines.

Before dark, before her parents get home from working, Kendall pulls herself out of bed and makes her way to the tool barn to collect the things she knows she'll need. She selects a flashlight, a shovel, and a hedge clipper and returns with them to her bedroom. She packs the items into a canvas sack and puts it under her bed.

She feels weak for lack of eating; too weak to try to find something to make her feel better. So she stays upstairs to dream about what will happen when she reunites with Nico. Soon. When her mother comes to check on her, Kendall says she's not feeling well.

She puts on her pajamas and pretends to turn in.

Come to me rings in her ears.

She doesn't sleep.

At eleven p.m., her parents sound asleep, Kendall rises from her bed. She picks up the sack. At the front window she stops. Lingers and says a last good-bye toward Nico's house. "See you soon," she whispers. And then, quietly, she sneaks out of the house. Locking the door behind her. Putting on her boots outside on the step.

A cold wind slaps her face and she can smell snow. The wind is a shock to her system, almost enough to make her brain kick into worry drive. Something nags at her, walking so freely, alone, like she's not supposed to be doing this, but she pushes the thought aside. She is going to save Nico now. This is her purpose. She says it under her breath as she walks, heel to toe, heel to toe. "Going to save Nico now. Going to save Nico now." Her eyes are on her boots as she trudges and trips in the dark.

Yet she walks determinedly through the field, staying off the road so she's not discovered. *Tell no one.* Twenty minutes later she lifts open the cellar door in the gravel behind the school. She steps down onto cracked concrete, her hair brushing low-hanging cobwebs, and walks past the storage room, where giant looming shadows of extra, unused desks taunt her. She climbs the interior steps that lead back up to the main level, and enters the classroom. She wipes a web from her face and stops in front of Nico's desk.

She shivers uncontrollably in her nightgown. For a split second she hesitates, her brain suddenly whirring about the time when she broke down while playing soccer with Jacián, after the last time she sat at Nico's desk. What if she's making a mistake?

"No!" she shouts in the dark room, shoving the memory aside. She has to save Nico—she has to. She brushes her fingers over the desk, teasingly, around the space where the graffiti changes, before she places her hand over it, absorbing its medicine. In the dark she can't read what it says, but the whispers tell her everything.

Harsh and wild, full of venom, the voice demands. The graffiti sears, electrocutes her fingers.

Find me before they kill me!
Deep in the woods
beyond Cryer's Pass.
Hurry! Save my soul!

Kendall gasps and whips her hand away, her fingers still burning. "Nico," she says to the harsh voice, "why are you talking to me like that?"

But there is no answer.

And he is in danger.

Kendall knows she must go.

She stumbles back downstairs, out the cellar door, and down the road. All of Cryer's Cross is asleep. Her nightgown whips around her body, the wind piercing through the thin fabric. Her feet are cold, bare inside her boots, and she begins to run, guided by newfound instinct, the voice inside her buzzing approval. She holds her bag of tools close to her chest. When she passes Hector's ranch, she turns to cut the corner, out of sight of his house, and then she heads down the path she took on horseback with Jacián. She follows the path for a short way until it branches, and then she takes the other branch and runs, runs as fast as she can, stumbling, teeth chattering, skin burning and itching from the wind. Her legs ache, unaccustomed to running in her boots.

After what seems like an hour at a solid jog, Kendall reaches Cryer's Pass, a road for quads and horses that winds up the ridge. Her side aches. Instead of taking the pass, she turns abruptly into the woods, still running, jumping over bushes and roots and vines until she trips and goes sprawling, landing on her bag. The hedge clippers pierce through the canvas and gouge a hole in her upper arm. She sits a moment, stunned, catching her breath, but there's no time to look at it, no time to stop the bleeding. Kendall gets back to her feet and staggers through the woods. "Nico!" she shouts. "Nico, where are you?"

She starts to run again, but soon running becomes impossible, so she presses on slowly, awkwardly, painfully, through brush and forest so thick that she nearly has to climb trees and swing from vines to get through. "Nico!" she screams. The voice in her head grows stronger. *Find me before he kills me! Thirty-five, one hundred!*

Her legs and arms sting from scratches. She stumbles

and catches herself, weak from not eating, strong from the voices that possess her. When she can go no farther, she pulls the clippers from the bag and starts tearing at ivy and branches, clipping and pulling them out of her way. She finds a spot that gives way. Squeezes and chops and pushes and clamps the clippers together until they clang against something metal. "Nico!" she screams. "Nico!"

WE

The heat, the life. Thirty-five, one hundred. Your heartbeat pounds in Our ears. "Come now!" We cry out, a piece of Us within you now. This victim, the most troublesome. Here. Now. Ready to redeem, release another lost soul. Thirty-five?

No.

ONE HUNDRED.

TWENTY-FOUR

She stumbles as she tries to slide through the slit she made in the ivy and vines between rusted iron rungs. She makes it through, finally, and scrambles to her feet, looking around in the eerie night glow.

There are fewer trees here. Smaller ones. And it's not quite so overgrown. With the light of a half-moon, Kendall makes out a large crumbling building away to her left, and a small broken-down shack nearer to her. She pulls out her flashlight and shines it around. She's in a sort of courtyard, but it's completely sealed off, even from the buildings, by an iron fence. Fog pockets rest in the valleys just beyond the yard. A bird squawks and settles. She hears the creaking of the trees, the rustling of other animals.

To the right, two dozen white markers stand in the ground. Kendall staggers, feeling herself being pulled toward them by the power of the voice inside her. She resists at first, confused, but then her body jerks into obedience. Her legs are heavy. She drags herself drunkenly across the dirt and brush.

The voice commands her. "Start digging," she whispers, startled, echoing it. "Start digging? Where? Where?" She pulls the shovel from her bag, and it leads her to the middle of the courtyard, where the crosses stand. "Nico!" she screams. "Where are you?" She has lost all control of her body. She pushes twigs and leaves aside with her boots, clearing a space.

Then she lifts the shovel and slams the point of it into the dirt in front of one of the markers. Her cold hands ache from the impact ricocheting off her bones, it seems, but she lifts and slams again, breaking the ground, beginning to dig, unable to stop herself. She piles the dirt carefully next to the hole and strikes again.

After a few minutes her punctured arm really hurts. Her hands shake. "Nico!" she calls out again. Her voice rings out, unanswered. She starts crying now, and screams louder for him, over and over as she piles the dirt high. Her back aches. She shivers, teeth rattling, and plunges the shovel into the hard dirt again. Again. Again.

* * *

When she hits bone, scooping a piece out with her shovel, she knows she has dug far enough. She knows now what she has to do, what the voice is forcing her to do in order to save Nico. She falls to her knees, hoarse but still screaming out his name. "I'm here to save you!" she cries. "Nico, help me!"

She sits down in the shallow grave she just dug. Reaches for the piles of dirt, drawing her arms around them and pulling them over her. Covering her feet and legs.

She watches herself in horror. Part of her can't believe she's doing it, and part of her can't get it done fast enough.

She is burying herself alive.

And she can't stop.

Slowly and methodically, simultaneously horrified and glorified by the process, she covers her body with dirt. She begins to chant. "Help me. Save my soul. Help me. Save my soul." Her chants turn to cries as she covers her thighs, her midsection. The dirt insulates her, warms her. Calms her shaking, but not her cries. She lies back and covers her chest. Her neck. She screams for Nico. Screams until her voice becomes muffled by the layer of dirt she pushes over her own face. All that remains aboveground is her hand.

And then—as the half-moon dips behind the broken-down building—all, everyone, everything is quiet once

again in the graveyard of the Cryer's Reform School for
Delinquent Boys.

A trapped soul waits for redemption.

It waits. And waits.

For her to take her last breath.

TWENTY-FIVE

It is still dark when the dirt stirs.

Kendall, struggling for air, feels something edging at her mind. She knows something feels terribly wrong about all of this. She knows from the voices that she must go through all of this to save Nico, but where is he? And how could this possibly help him? Her OCD brain churns, and the single thought slips in. *This is wrong. This is wrong.* She starts to count now. Counts the heartbeats, counts the pebbles in her mouth, counts the minutes as they pass. Some of the fog in her head clears. Enough. Just enough. Enough to struggle.

The grasp, the hold of the voice weakens. Just enough. And with Kendall's one remaining free arm, she pushes the layer of dirt from her face, spits out the gravel from her mouth, and gives one last rasping cry before she passes out. "Jacián."

The voice in her head—not Nico's, never Nico's—cries out as if in pain.

TWENTY-SIX

In the morning it rains.

The water washes dirt from her eyes.

The voice remains, crying out to her, but she knows now that it's not Nico. She fights the voice with her own weapon, her own tool. The whirring thoughts are welcomed. She holds the power.

She can't move at first. The rain makes the grave cover like a straitjacket, like wide belts holding her in. She can only turn her head. Cough the dirt out.

In the rainy morning light she sees more clearly now. Thinks more clearly. The markers, white crosses. The bones her boots are touching are old. This place, so forlorn. Abandoned. Stuck in a different time. The only sound is rain on leaves, rain on dirt, rain on skin.

All the events of the previous day start coming back to her as she surfaces and takes back control of her senses. Clears the fuzz in her brain. "Oh my God!" she cries out. "What is happening?" She panics and begins to struggle. The horror of what nearly happened, the claustrophobia, being submerged in wet dirt, gives her the superhuman strength she needs to push out from under it. She grips the side of the grave and pulls, heaves herself to her stomach, coughing.

Her throat hurts and she's freezing, filthy, covered in scratches and bruises. She lifts her head and looks around the overgrown yard, seeing all the crosses now.

Twenty-four of them.

Lined up in four equal quadrants.

With aisles between each section.

In the two spots next to Kendall, the dirt is somewhat fresher. Raised up. She looks closer and sees a decomposing hand sticking out from one and bones from the other. She crawls to the one closest and starts digging.

Long brown hair comes away in her hand—it's not Nico. Could it be Tiffany?

Kendall becomes increasingly aware of the stench in the graveyard.

She dry heaves off to the side, and crawls over to the other grave. Looks at the decomposing hand, wipes her eyes and looks again. The tissue wavers before her eyes. And then she sees why.

Maggots.

She turns, gagging from the sight and smell, gagging again from all the dirt drying out her throat.

She begins digging with what little strength she has left, her fingers bleeding. "Please no, please no, please no," she cries softly, over and over.

She scrapes the dirt away. Brushes it from his black, bloated face, his white-blond hair confirming her worst fear.

"No!" Her cry rasps from deep inside her chest. She falls away onto her back, sobbing, until she has nothing else left. She rolls as far away as she can before she's too exhausted to move.

She lies there, quiet, no longer feeling cold or pain. No longer caring.

Nico is dead.

As the rain slows and the hours tick forward into evening, there is a noise.

"Kendall!" she hears. It seems so far away.

She is delusional. Too weak to shout. "Nico?" She rasps. Rain puddles around her. Everything is dark.

Someone picks her up, wraps a coat around her, carries

her like a baby. She hears more voices far away, exclaiming in horror.

They move quickly. A branch slaps her face, and she startles.

"Shit, sorry," he says.

"Jacián," she whispers. Her chest sears in pain with every breath. She struggles in his arms.

"Sit tight. We've got a ways to go."

"They're dead."

"Yes." He jiggles her as he breaks into a jog, leaving the thickest woods behind. And eventually, back on the path at Cryer's Pass, he hoists her up onto his four-runner and glides in next to her, holding her around the shoulders, helping her sit up. Takes off toward the ranch. "I'm sorry," he says. "It's going to be bumpy here for a bit."

"How did you find me?" She leans into him, too cold to shiver. Too tired to open her eyes. Her throat feels like she swallowed broken glass.

He pulls the coat tightly around her and holds her as he drives. His mouth is close, warm near her ear. "They called the search first thing this morning when your parents noticed you were gone, around five. Soon after, everybody rolled into town. We're getting too good at this." He adjusts his grip on Kendall's shoulder and steps on the gas as they approach a clearing.

"I remembered what you said about the desk," he continues. "Yeah, it was weird, but I would have tried anything at that point. I'm so pissed at myself for not . . . Oh hell, never mind." He scowls, but she doesn't see it. "So, anyway, I went to school to look for clues. Old Mr. Greenwood let me in. I sat at the desk, read all the graffiti. In the middle it said 'Deep in the woods beyond Cryer's Pass.' I almost didn't think it would mean anything because the carvings looked so old, but I mentioned it to my grandfather, and he almost fainted. He called the sheriff and old Mr. Greenwood. They took the truck out here, but it got caught in the vines trying to drive over. So we're going this way."

His voice sounds far away, and the voice of the desk doesn't leave her. Everything in her brain is mud. "Don't let them bury me," she says.

"Oh, Kendall." His voice breaks. "Did somebody do this to you? Did anyone touch you?"

She shakes her head. "No. It's just the voices. They made me . . . do things. . . ." She lets a sob escape, and then explodes into a racking cough.

"Voices? You mean . . . ," he says slowly, "you heard something, when you touched the desk?"

"Yes, the voices." Kendall grips her throat as it burns.

"Shh . . . You can explain once we get you to the hospital."

They reach Hector's ranch, and Jacián pulls the quad up next to the barn. He carries Kendall to his truck, starts it up to get the heat flowing, and then picks up the barn phone to make a quick call to Kendall's parents.

"I've got her. She's alive. I'm taking her to Bozeman Hospital. It's faster than waiting on an ambulance. Is that okay? . . . Good. She's talking, but she's been out in the rain all night and day."

He listens for a moment and then says, "See you there."

He rushes into the truck and takes off down the road, the heater on full blast. He slides Kendall over to him and cradles his arm around her. Halfway to Bozeman she's shivering. Jacián says that's a good sign.

He pulls up to the emergency room and carries her inside, grabbing an empty wheelchair and the first person in scrubs that he sees. "Hey, man, she's freezing. Soaking wet," he says, setting Kendall down in the wheelchair. The orderly hesitates, glances at the waiting room and then at Kendall's blue lips, and takes her away. Someone at the desk hands Jacián a clipboard with forms on it. He stares at it blankly. Carries it to the entrance to meet Mr. and Mrs. Fletcher. Tells them everything he knows as they fill out the paperwork.

For a moment Jacián just stands there looking down the long, bustling hallway, thinking, catching his breath before it all catches up to him. And then he turns and goes out to park the truck.

And to get a grip on things before he loses it.

TWENTY-SEVEN

It's pneumonia, probably some dirt inhaled into her lungs, and the cold rain didn't help. Kendall spends the first day with a high fever, in and out of consciousness. Not caring what is happening, only mourning around the edges of reality. Her best friend in all the world, the boy who knew her best, the guy who wanted to be a nurse so he could help people feel better, is dead. And he died in a horrible way.

Part of her knew he had to be dead. When Eli said it at the Obregons' party, she believed he was probably right. But the desk . . . his voice. It's still killing her.

When she wakes up, her mother is there, reading by the bed, her half-glasses near the tip of her nose. There's another bed in the room, but it's empty.

"Hey, Mom," Kendall says in a gravelly voice, and cringes. There are oxygen tubes in her nostrils, and her throat is raw, burning. An IV is attached to one arm, and stitches poke from the other where the clippers stabbed her. Her legs and arms, even her stomach is covered with scratches and bruises.

Mrs. Fletcher sits up quickly, puts her book on the table, and a smile spreads across her face. "Kendall," she says. "How's my girl?"

Kendall points to her throat and makes a sad face.

Mrs. Fletcher reaches for a glass of water and feeds the straw into Kendall's mouth.

Kendall sucks on the straw, feeling the cool water soothe her throat.

"Do you want a pen and some paper?" Mrs. Fletcher rummages through her purse.

Kendall doesn't have any energy to write, but then she nods anyway. Why not? Turns out she has a few burning questions, once she's fully awake.

"Nico died," she writes.

Mrs. Fletcher presses her fingers to her lips as she thinks about how to say things. "They're both . . . dead. Did you know that?"

Kendall nods. Tears well up in her eyes. She knew it, but hearing her mother say it out loud makes it feel true.

"They're exhuming the bodies for autopsy. The Quinns

and the Cruzes are going to have proper burials and a memorial service in the cemetery behind the church in a few days. And now everybody's trying to find out who murdered them, who buried them there. And why. Honey," Mrs. Fletcher says in earnest, her voice filled with worry and dread, "do you remember who did this to you? How did you . . . he . . ." She can't say it. "The police are going to talk to you again." Her voice breaks, and she grabs a tissue.

Kendall isn't sure what to say. She writes on her notepad, "I don't really remember anything." She doesn't like lying, but if she tells the truth, she knows they'll put her away.

Mrs. Fletcher reaches down and hugs Kendall tightly. "It's okay, baby. Just tell the police what you remember and that's all you have to do."

Kendall nods.

When Sheriff Greenwood comes, he brings a small entourage with him—old Mr. Greenwood and Hector Morales, who stand outside the door to her room, not looking in.

"I brought you some visitors if you're up for it," the sheriff says to Kendall.

Kendall nods.

"Mrs. Fletcher, can I speak to you in private?"

"Of course." Mrs. Fletcher gives Kendall's knee a comforting squeeze through the blankets. Then she follows the sheriff.

When the two go off to the waiting room to talk, Hector and old Mr. Greenwood enter Kendall's room. It's weird to have them here.

"Miss Kendall," Hector says. He holds his cowboy hat in hand. "I'm so sorry for your pain."

Kendall nods, saving her voice.

"How are you?"

She shrugs. Whispers, "Okay."

"This seems strange, doesn't it? But we are here for good reason. I need to tell you a story about one of my friends."

Puzzled, Kendall just looks at them, from one face to the other, wondering what's up. She nods and points at the chairs, inviting them to sit.

Once settled, Hector glances tentatively at old Mr. Greenwood, who sits down in the other bedside chair. He presses his lips together in a white line and stares at the floor.

Hector weaves his fingers together in his lap and gazes into his cupped hands as if he's searching for the right words to spill forth. And then, after a few false starts, he tells a story from a long time ago. A story about a boy named Piere who was sent to live at the Cryer's Reform School for Delinquent Boys.

He tells about the poor conditions there, and the terrible treatment the boys received, how one night this boy Piere had to sleep on his stomach because his back was in shreds, oozing with blood and pus from being whipped by the headmaster. How Piere's best friend, Samuel, was sent for a whipping the next night, and Piere snuck out to the little white shack to watch through the crack in the door, knowing that if he were caught, he'd be punished again. But not caring. He needed to be there for his friend.

Piere watched the headmaster, Horace Cryer, bring down the whip again and again on Samuel's back and thighs as the boy braced himself, back arched, over the whipping desk. He watched Samuel's welts grow and turn grayish purple, the blood just under the skin, and then exploding red on the next hit when the skin broke, the blood spraying through the air, all over the walls.

Piere counted, knowing there were only two kinds of beatings from Mr. Cryer. Thirty-five lashes for minor disobedience. One hundred for everything else . . . and sometimes for no reason at all.

When Mr. Cryer didn't stop at thirty-five, Piere's stomach clenched. After several more lashes, the silent Samuel let out a bloodcurdling scream, which only drove Mr. Cryer to bring the whip down harder. Piere watched as Samuel's elbows slipped off the desk, his chest and cheek smashing against it, beads of blood on his lower lip. He watched his friend's eyes roll back and close.

Piere clutched his shirt in agony, tearing his own oozing sores open again, and then he stumbled blindly away, back to his bunk.

He never saw Samuel again.

Hector looks up at Kendall. She's gripping the bed sheets, staring at him. The eerie numbers, thirty-five and one hundred. The whipping desk . . . She tries to say something, chokes, drinks some water and tries again. "That's a horrible story," she says. "Is it true?"

Hector nods. "Yes. I am sorry I had to tell it."

"Is that place . . . is that where I was?"

"Yes."

She bites her lip, thinking about Samuel. "You talked about a desk."

Hector's eyes glisten. His face screws up in anger, remorse. He nods. "The whipping desk. All the desks in your classroom came from the reform school. The state brought them over when they opened your school."

Kendall just stares.

"And when Jacián told me what you said when he found you . . . I am not superstitious," he says, shaking his finger, "but I knew they should have left it there to rot. There was evil there in that place, on those grounds. Evil in the heart of Horace Cryer."

Old Mr. Greenwood sits stone-faced, listening like he

can hardly bear to hear it, denying nothing.

"Mr. Cryer beat us all multiple times over that desk," Hector says. "Many of our friends were murdered by him. We didn't know what he did with the bodies. We weren't allowed beyond the gate. But now we know . . . now we know. There are so many crosses."

Hector pulls a handkerchief from his coat pocket and mops his face with it, grieving all over again. "You have to understand, we had no one. All of us either orphans or abandoned as hopeless delinquents, like me. Who would listen to us? We never talked about it, never told anyone. We only wanted to forget." He dabs the corners of his eyes. "Make new lives once we got out."

Kendall remains silently horrified as she tries to comprehend. The souls of the dead boys . . . beaten into the desk? Trapped there, angry, their business undone . . . stuck away in storage all these years, only to be set free whenever they found a body to go into? It was impossible. No one would believe it. Yet here she was, with two of the most respected people of Cryer's Cross, and neither was denying it.

"We know about the voice," old Mr. Greenwood says abruptly, surprising everyone. Then he glances at Kendall, measuring her. "If you repeat this, I will deny it. But I have heard the whisper too."

Kendall's eyes spring open wide. "You have?"

He nods and looks back at the floor, as if he can't look her in the eye. "I didn't know where it came from. Didn't pay attention to that desk in particular as I shoved the desks around." He wipes his eyes with his hand. "Thirty-five, one hundred, buzzing around my ears, those numbers taunting me. I thought it was me. I thought I was going senile. Post-traumatic stress or something. The voice sounded like . . . like Samuel."

"It said things to me in Nico's voice," Kendall whispers. "Tiffany and Nico both sat at that desk."

"Yes, Jacián told me. We've pieced it together," Hector says. "He said he heard whispers when he touched it too." Hector looks up, out the open door to the empty hallway. "The sheriff will be coming back soon. He knows of our hunch about the desk, but he doesn't know what to believe, doesn't want to commit to a story so unnatural. I don't blame him—two old coots like us with a crazy hunch. But we're going to remove that desk. Not to worry."

Kendall nods. "Thank you." She is flooded with relief, so glad she is no longer alone in this.

"He's going to ask you what you remember. It's up to you what you want to say when he asks you questions. But as far as the people of Cryer's Cross and the national news networks know, we're all now looking for an elusive kidnapper and murderer." He pauses, and his voice softens. "Maybe it's best, for your sake, if it stays that way."

Kendall sinks back into the pillows, feeling a little light-headed.

When the sheriff comes in with Mrs. Fletcher, Hector smiles at Kendall and squeezes her hand.

"Thank you for visiting, gentlemen," Mrs. Fletcher says to the men. "It means a lot that you came to see her."

Hector tips his hat. "Miss Kendall is a special girl, a good friend to me and my grandchildren," he says, old eyes shining. "She is like family." He gets to his feet, and old Mr. Greenwood moves to do the same. Hector looks at him and holds out a hand. "Ready?"

"I don't need your help," Old Mr. Greenwood grumbles.

TWENTY-EIGHT

She told the sheriff that she didn't remember anything, only that she felt like she'd been drugged, not in control of her actions. Tests couldn't confirm any drugs in her body, but the reporters got anonymously tipped off nonetheless.

She sits in the hospital still, three days later, the small stream of visitors having dissipated. The local TV news is on, and Kendall is watching people arrive for the burial service for Nico and Tiffany. It's a big deal for southwest Montana. It'd be a big deal anywhere. Maybe seventy or eighty strangers mill around the grave site, those oddities who'd gotten sucked in by the story and feel, in some unexplainable way, connected to the two missing teens. It's weird to see them. But even weirder to see people she knows and sees every day, standing so solemnly, all dressed up. She sees Nico's and Tiffany's extended families up front, the camera invading their grief.

She sees her own parents, looking older than what she thinks them to be. She sees the Greenwoods and the Shanks arriving with some of the other people of Cryer's Cross, and she's struck by how horribly often the little town has had to gather all at once like this over the past five months, stopping everything for another tragedy, then trudging onward with life.

The caskets hang suspended over the graves in plot sections that have no patriarchs, no matriarchs. Teenagers aren't supposed to die. Kendall pulls an extra pillow to her chest and hugs it, wondering why on earth she convinced her mother to go to the memorial and leave her here alone during this.

She sees Hector and the Obregons. Marlena in a black dress, Jacián in a dark suit with a white shirt, no tie. They find seats, and Jacián jiggles his foot up and down as they wait for it to begin. And finally it does.

A few minutes into it, the TV news anchor cuts in and brings breaking news of something else, a fire downtown or something, and the service is gone. Kendall turns off the TV and stares at the ceiling, remembering Nico in her own private way. His smile, the light in his eyes. How he'd do anything for her, and she for him.

She thinks about their romance, how it came as a by-product, an experiment in their friendship. Their parents always talked about them being together forever. It was just a given as they grew up.

She thinks about how she never really felt comfortable calling him her boyfriend until after he was gone. He was in love with her, she knew. But she just loved him. It wasn't the same. He was such a good person that she knew she should be in love with him. Who wouldn't? But there was no passion. It was sweet, she realizes now, and that's all it was. She thinks about what was special with them. How kissing him wasn't all that important. But loyalty? Loyalty was everything.

The tears stream down her face for the goodness that Nico was. For the memories she will never forget. For all the times he stood up for her, the only girl in their class, and for all the times she beat him honestly, at soccer or tests or a footrace down to the river. She cries for all the people he won't get to help, for the diploma he'll never earn, for his parents and family, who will never be the same again. For the hole in her heart left by the loss of a best friend.

And then she cries for the way he died. She knows what he went through, and she can only hope he was so under the influence of the possessed souls in the desk that he didn't know what horror he was doing to himself. She wonders whose voice he heard. Maybe it was Tiffany's. He'd be the guy to want to save someone in trouble, there's no doubt about that. She'll never know the answer to that one.

It was the OCD that saved her. She knows that. And as much as she hates how it rules and ruins her everyday life, she vows that she will never complain about it again.

She's sitting up in a chair, showered and slightly exhausted from the effort, but still wishing she could just bust out of the hospital—when the phone rings. She shuffles over to it and answers, her voice still husky but no longer sore from all the beatings it took.

"Hello," she says.

"Hey."

Her stomach twists. "Hey . . . How are you?"

It's quiet on the line, and for a minute Kendall thinks Jacián might have hung up. But then he speaks. "I'm fine. I'm . . . I just wondered if you were doing okay. Is this a bad time?"

"No. I mean, yes, I'm doing okay. No, it's not a bad time." She sits down on the edge of the bed. "I saw you on TV, at the memorial service. . . ."

"Yeah?"

"Yeah, it wasn't on for long before they cut to the next tragedy, though. You looked nice."

"Thanks. Look, Kendall?" he sounds anxious.

"Yes?"

"I'm sorry to bother you. I know this is a tough time for you, with Nico and all, and you probably don't want to see me. But I've just been thinking about you . . . God. All the time. Do you mind if I come up to your room?"

Kendall blinks. "Where are you?"

"In the lobby." He sounds miserable.

Kendall's stomach drops to the floor. She swallows hard. "I look . . . pretty terrible. Bruises, scratches . . . I guess you've seen that already, though."

"If you don't want me to come up, that's cool. It was just an impulsive thing. I went for a drive after the service and ended up here. I can go."

"No! I mean, please. Come up. I was just, you know, warning you. I'm in four sixteen."

There is silence. An intake of breath. And then, "I'm on the way."

Kendall hangs up the phone. She dashes to the bathroom and checks her hair, shakes it in front of her face to try to hide the scratches, but it only makes her look worse, so she smoothes it back again. She slips into her robe. A moment later she hears a soft knock on the door.

She takes a deep breath and opens it.

He walks in.

Stands there hesitantly for a minute, still wearing his

suit from the memorial service, shirt untucked, black hair disheveled from the wind. He takes her in from toe to head. His eyes land on hers and stay there. And he says softly, "You don't look terrible."

Her stomach flips over, scares her.

He goes to her, opens his arms, and she wraps hers around his neck, feels the chill of the evening on his jacket.

They hold each other gently, thoughts rushing through their minds, memories of when he found her. She buries her face in his neck. "Thank you for saving my life," she says. "That was really scary." From nowhere and everywhere, the sobs come.

He runs his hand over her hair and swallows hard. "You did it yourself," he says. "I don't know how you did that. How you did what Tiffany and Nico couldn't do. But you saved yourself," he murmurs. "You did it. All you."

"I would have frozen to death out there without you."

He holds her tighter. "I'm so sorry," he whispers. He presses his lips to her hair.

Everything inside her body melts.

She is chocolate in his fist.

WE

We scream but the noise is lost. No listeners remain. A sliver of Us is gone, trapped, dormant inside the life. Ancient heat hovers at the edges of Our face, manhandling Us, bumping and shoving, away, away. Perhaps now We will find heat, life anew. We settle. And once again, We wait.

TWENTY-NINE

She's nervous her first day going back to school. She waits by the cold window, fogging it up with her breath, until she sees the truck. Then she kisses her mother and father good-bye. They wave and go back to their newspapers and coffee—a small reward, a luxury for another harvest completed.

Jacián pushes the door open for her from the inside, and she hops in. He turns the truck around and takes off down the driveway.

"Where's Marlena?"

"She's been hitching a ride with Eli the past few days. They hung out after the memorial service, and I think maybe they've got a little thing going." He glances sidelong at her.

She grins. "How cool! Eli's a sweet guy. That's perfect."

He shrugs. "I don't know. Little things are overrated if you ask me."

"I see."

"Yeah, it's sort of all or nothing with me. Yep."

Kendall's eyes narrow. "I'm feeling an urge to smack you again."

"Ooh," he says. He slows the truck.

"No! We have to get to school. No time for that now."

"Right. My bad."

"Please just tell me somebody straightened the desks while I was gone."

"Sure. I did."

"You did that for me?"

He looks at her like she's nuts. "Um . . . no. I'm not that good."

"Oh. Ha, ha." Kendall takes a deep breath and lets it out. "God, I'm nervous to go back in there."

Jacián pulls into the parking lot, takes her hand, kisses it, and peers at her through his thick lashes. "You can do it."

It's weird being here again. She walks in and looks around. Turns the wastebasket, straightens the markers. Opens the curtains and checks the locks, whispering, "All checked and good."

Then she looks at the desks.

They're all there. Twenty-four of them. She breaks from her usual pattern and goes first to the senior section. Stops at Nico's place. Jacián watches her quietly.

"It's a different desk," she says.

"Yes."

"I've never seen this one before." She draws her fingers across the graffiti carefully, ready to pull back at the first whisper. But nothing happens. It's just a desk. "I'm glad they replaced it. It would look wrong if there was a hole in this spot."

"I mentioned that," Jacián says. He walks over to her. "It's from the storage room. I said I thought it would be less conspicuous to the other students if they put a new one here, that you and I would be the only ones who noticed the switch."

She nods, deep in thought. She turns, searching his face, his eyes. "Hector says you heard the whispers too."

He nods. "I did. I thought it was my mind messing with me. But then I remembered the way you wrapped yourself around the desk whenever you sat there." He touches her arm. "I held my hand to it for longer than I want to admit. I couldn't stop. It almost had me too, Kendall."

Kendall bites her lip. "Whose voice did you hear?"

He swallows hard. Touches her face. "Yours."

* * *

After school Jacián and Kendall drive to the church graveyard. Little bits of snow fall to the graying ground. Kendall gets out of the truck and walks slowly to the grave site, Jacián holding back, giving her some space. She stares at the fresh dirt and shudders with cold and memories, memories of his decomposing face that she knows she'll never forget.

She fights the demanding thoughts that want to swirl around her head. Instead she forces new ones, remembering the good times with the best friend anybody could ever have. She beckons over her shoulder and reaches for Jacián, threads her arm around his waist. He slips his hand to her shoulder, absently weaving his fingers through her hair as they silently pay their respects together.

She is out of tears.

She kneels by the grave as the snow falls on it. Closes her eyes and pictures him, long blond hair swishing around his head, that grin. She smiles back at him. "I'll miss you," she whispers. "Good-bye, Nico."

At Hector's that evening, Jacián and Kendall sit around the table with a computer and catalogs, researching.

"There's NYU's Tisch in New York," Jacián says. "Or FSU Dance. That's Florida. What about Hartford?"

Kendall pages through the options. "There's a lot of dance schools," she admits.

"San Diego, Ohio, or hey, maybe University of Arizona. That's down where we used to live."

"No potatoes?"

Jacián smiles. "No potatoes. Lemons, limes, avocados. Horses nearby."

"I like horses. Hate potatoes."

He squeezes her thigh. "You'll have a lot of excellent choices once you pull your grades up again."

Kendall sighs. "Yeah. I guess spending all that time ignoring everything wasn't such a good idea, grade-wise."

"Hey," he says. He turns her chin so he can look into her eyes. "You survived it."

She nods.

"Let's go take a break."

They slip their jackets on and step out onto the porch. It's bone cold outside. Jacián leans against the railing and pulls Kendall to him. He kisses her softly. She leans into him and holds him, feeling the shape of his body through his shirt, his heartbeat against hers. She counts the beats lazily, more as a comfort than a compulsion.

"I smell a bonfire," Kendall says after a while.

"Mmm-hmm."

"Want to walk? Go check it out?"

"Sure."

They walk hand in hand until they can see the flames, hear the crackle. Hector and old Mr. Greenwood hold shovels. The firelight against their bodies makes huge jumping shadows along the tree line behind them. The carcass of the desk stands on metal legs, fire licking, angry smoke erupting from it.

Jacián and Kendall approach with caution, and then they watch, silent alongside the solemn-faced men thinking about the boys who died on that desk so many years ago, and the students who died this year because of it.

Kendall clears her throat. "Whatever happened to the boy in the story? Piere?" she asks.

Hector pulls himself from his thoughts and glances at old Mr. Greenwood, who frowns mightily at the fire. "He made it," Hector says softly. "He did himself proud."

When the wooden desktop collapses in on itself and shudders in the ashes, Kendall feels a rush of cold escape her lungs and hears a faint drawn-out scream.

But then it's gone again.

WE

We feel the heat, and for a moment, We believe! Life is back. But this heat is intense, not gentle. Not submissive but searing. Painful.

We moan, scream, Our face cracking like gunfire . . . like a whip. Thirty-five, one hundred. One hundred! ONE HUNDRED!

The fire consumes Our wooden host. It burns, breaks, explodes. Releases Our remaining souls to travel to Our final resting places.

Or.

To find new places to hide.

And wait.

Touch me.

ONE

There are three of them. No, four.

They step off the Amtrak train into the snowy dusk, children first and adults after, and then they hesitate, clustered on the platform. Passengers behind them shove past, but the four—Blake, Gracie, Dad, Mama—just move a few more steps and stop again, look around. Their faces are an uneasy yellow in the overhead light from the station. Mama looks most anxious. She peers into the darkness under the awning where I stand, just twenty feet away, as if she knows instinctively that I am here, but no confirmation registers on her face. I am still invisible in the shadows.

Invisible, but cornered. Backed up against the station wall, next to a bench, the woman from Child Protective Services whom I met this afternoon standing beside me. It's too late to stop this now. Too late to go back, too late to run away. I press my back into the wall, feeling the tenderness of a recent bruise on my right shoulder blade. I wet my chapped lips and break into a cold sweat.

"Is that them?" the woman asks quietly.

"It's them," I say. And I'm sure. I feel panic welling up in my gut.

If I move, they'll see me.

TWO

I take a deep breath, hold it, and force myself to step out from under the awning into the yellow light. Walk toward them. Mama sees me, and her mittened hand clutches her coat where it opens at her neck. As I approach, I can see her eyes shining above deep gray semicircles, and I can tell she's not sure—I'm not seven anymore. Her lips part and I imagine she gasps a bit. Then Dad, Blake, and finally Gracie, the replacement child, stare with doubting eyes, taking me in.

I open my mouth to say something, but I don't know what to say. It's almost like the cold sweat in the small of my back, in my armpits, freezes me in place.

Mama takes Dad's arm and they stumble over to me while the two children hang back. And then they're right in front of me, and I'm looking into Mama's eyes.

"Ethan?" she says within a visible exhaled breath that envelopes me, then dissipates. She touches my hair, my cheek. Her breath smells like spearmint, and her eyes fill up with tears. Her skin is darker, and she's rounder, shorter than I expected. A lot shorter than me. I stand almost even with my dad, which feels right. Like I belong with this group of people.

I'm surprised to find tears welling in my own eyes. I haven't cried in a while, but it feels good to be with them. All at once, I feel wanted.

"It's really you," she says, wonder in her voice. She throws herself at me, sobs into my neck, and I close my eyes and hold her and let out a breath.

"Mama," I whisper into her soft hair. I am at once sixteen, my actual age, and seven, the age they remember me. We are long-lost souls, a mother reuniting with her semi-prodigal son. It is the end of one story and the beginning of the next.

Being near her makes my teeth stop chattering.

THREE

Dad comes in for a group hug, and we are suddenly stepping on each other's feet, not sure where to put our heads in the crowded space. I turn my face outward and see Blake watching. We hold each other's gaze for several seconds, until my eyes cross from staring, and I think, for a moment, that he looks a little bit like this yellow dog I used to see hanging around the group home. He really does. I close my eyes.

The woman from CPS gently interrupts, lays a hand on my coat sleeve. I pull away from my parents. "Ethan," she says, "I'm sorry to intrude. It seems obvious, but I need to ask a few questions." We nod, and she looks at me. "Are these your parents?"

I'm choked up, but I say in a weird voice, "Yes, ma'am."

She asks my parents for identification and they fumble in an attempt to show it as quickly as possible. Asks them officially, "Is this your son?"

Mama breaks down. "Yes," she says, sobbing. "Finally. I can't believe it. Thank you. Thank you so much."

"Please don't be offended by the next question—I'm required to ask. Would you like a DNA test?"

They look at each other and then at me. "Absolutely not," Mama says. "I'm positive."

"There's no need for that," Dad says.

There are a few more questions and papers for them to sign, so we step out of the snow, into the building. At a closed ticket window we spread things out on the ledge, and that's all there is. I already talked to the cops this afternoon. There are no more formalities. It's almost like I got lost in the fishing tackle aisle of Wal-Mart for ten minutes. *This your mom? This your kid? Good. Stay close now, keep a better eye out.*

The woman from CPS squeezes my arm, searches my eyes, and apparently sees what she wants in them—enough to satisfy her that I am okay with all of this. She puts her hand to her chest and says, "Congratulations to all of you." Her voice fills out, like she's choking up. "It's really such an amazing, joyful event when one of the lost ones makes it home again." She smiles brightly, but her eyes glisten. I figure it must feel good to her, like they actually finished a job. To me, it just feels like nausea.

Then the woman turns businesslike. "Mr. and Mrs. De Wilde, we've arranged for our counselor, Dr. Cook, to talk with you all and explain what we know. The train station manager was kind enough to let us use the break room to do this. Ethan, would you like me to stay?" She ushers us to the room and opens the door.

I shake my head. "No, that's okay." It only gets worse the longer she stays. I can't even remember her name, I'm so anxious. Dr. Cook is sitting inside at a round table. I talked to her this afternoon. She has six pencils stuck in the ball of hair at the back of her head—four yellows, two reds.

"All right." The CPS woman steps in after us and introduces my family to Dr. Cook. "Good luck, Ethan," she says. "I'll be in touch in a day or two to see how it's going."

I nod.

Dr. Cook smiles at Blake. "Maybe you and your little sister can sit outside in the waiting area."

Blake glances at Mama and scowls. Mama says, "Yes, good idea."

They go. We sit. And Dr. Cook debriefs.

It's a relief, it really is, to have her talk to my parents instead of me. She tells them everything I told her. Which, when you think of it, really isn't much at all. I have three seasons of my life that I want to forget now that I'm here: Ellen (I told them her name was Eleanor—I don't know why), group home, and homeless. My mind wanders and my eyes roam the break room, land on the countertop. Spilled sugar. Coffee stains. A mug with a unicorn on it. For a minute I stare at it, thinking it moved, but it didn't—I'm just tired. The coffeepot with the orange lid means decaf. I know that from the breakfast place Ellen worked at once in a while, whenever she needed the money. The little bit of coffee left in the pot is starting to burn and I can't look at it. The smell is sharp in my nose. The doctor says, "About two years ago, Eleanor abandoned him in Omaha at a group home." She tells them how I ran away from there and lived at the park and around the zoo. I blow breath out of my nose to get the burned smell out. Finally I just get up and turn off the burner. Dad gives me a curious look, but I don't care. I just don't think having this place burn down right now would make things easier.

Dr. Cook gives Mama the business card of a psychologist who lives near us. Says we should go individually and as a family. All these details are making me twitchy.

When Dr. Cook leaves, we walk out of the break room and find Gracie hopping around the waiting area, babbling about kindergarten, and Blake sitting on the floor against the wall, staring at the ceiling.

"Well, it's official," Mama says with a huge smile, and hugs me again. When she finally lets go, Dad is next. Slaps me hard on the back, right near where my shoulder hurts. I hide a wince and take it like a man.

Blake stands up but doesn't hug me. He stays back, shuffles his feet, embarrassed by absolutely everything. And the girl, the replacement child, she just stares at me.

It's both jubilant and awkward, the five of us all wondering and staring and trying not to get caught looking. Mama apologizes for not bringing balloons. There wasn't time to do anything, she says, and I believe her, since I just called CPS once I made it into Minnesota this morning. They really high-tailed it down here, actually. Must have. And I'm glad for that. I'm grateful. I look around the station, noticing other people for the first time, all of them busy trying to get home, I bet.

We have celebratory hot chocolate from an ancient, faded machine, waiting for the train that will take us home together, a complete family. Dad excuses himself after a minute and I watch him at the ticket counter, buying one more ticket home. My ticket. And I wonder, have they done this before? They didn't want to waste the money in case I wasn't me?

Everyone tries a little too hard. The small talk is strained. Gracie, who's six according to the family website, judges me from a safe distance behind Mama, who is talking excitedly on the phone. Talking about me. I take a sip of my hot chocolate too soon, and now my tongue feels like burlap.

Blake stares at my feet. He was there when it happened—the only witness. Just two brothers drawing with chalk on the sidewalk in front of the house, innocent as can be. I wonder if he remembers it. He doesn't say much. He just glances at me once in a while when he thinks I'm not looking.

"I can't believe it," Mama says over and over to me between

calls. "You're all grown up. Such a little boy, and now you're all grown up."

Dad's quiet. He wipes his face with a white handkerchief that he keeps balled up in his hand.

A few times I try to ask a question, but I always change my mind right before I say anything. The words don't sound right. What am I supposed to say? *So, is it always this cold in Minnesota? Or, Hey, what have you guys been doing for the past nine years? I see you got busy replacing me.*

On the train it's even harder. We sit in two rows that face each other. I'm by the window, next to Blake. Mama and Dad sit across from us, with Gracie between them. I hold my beat-up old bag on my lap to keep it safe from the slush on the floor. It's so difficult for me to look them in the eyes, like if I do I'm committing to something, even though I'm dying to take in their faces. To get a better picture. They are all looking at me, paying attention to me, asking me simple questions, and actually, I like that. I do. It makes me feel like something.

When there's a lull, I rack my brains for something to say, and I remember the photos on the website. "Still the same old house?" I feel myself starting to sweat again.

Dad clears his throat. "Still the same, yep. Thirty-fifth and Maple." He pauses. "Do you remember it?" His voice is gentle, careful.

"Some of it," I say, careful too. I know it only from the pictures on the website, but I don't want to hurt his feelings. "The front steps and the sidewalk and the white cement driveway, with the grass growing in the cracks. The Christmas tree in the big picture window, and a little black dog—what was his name?" I screw up my eyes, pretending to try to remember, but I already know that I don't know the dog's name. I see the photo of him in my head, but there are so many questions.

"Rags," Mama says with a smile. "Rags died a couple years after . . . about six years ago. Right around when Gracie was born."

"I'm sorry," I say. "He was a nice dog."

Dad laughs. "You hated that dog. He always chewed on your shoes."

"Really?" I laugh too, a little too hard. "I don't remember that."

A few weeks ago, at the library, I found the page—my face staring back at me. My page, with my real name—Ethan Manuel De Wilde—on the National Center for Missing & Exploited Children's website. I Googled my name and saw all the hits. People had been looking for me. Unreal. And then I found my family's website. Even Grandpa and Grandma De Wilde and all the cousins and aunts and uncles post things there. Tons of pictures. Discussions about them . . . and about me. How they've been searching, and how they remember. Memories shared.

Things flash by the window and in my head: sleeping in

doorways, the group home in Nebraska, and how I got there . . .
and Ellen. . . . My throat hurts. I stare outside into the darkness,
watching glowing snow and bare black trees whiz by.

"Um, so, what else do you remember, Ethan?" Blake asks
after a while, still not quite looking at me. His voice is non-
chalant, but I know what he's really asking. He's asking, *Do you
remember me?*

ABOUT THE AUTHOR

Lisa McMann is the author of the *New York Times* bestselling Wake trilogy, *Dead to You*, and the middle-grade dystopian fantasy series The Unwanteds. She lives with her family in the Phoenix area. Read more about Lisa and find her blog through her website at LisaMcMann.com or, better yet, find her on Facebook (facebook.com/mcmannfan) or follow her on Twitter (twitter.com/lisa_mcmann).